CANDLELIGHT REGENCY SPECIAL

LA CASA
DORADA

Janet Louise Roberts

A CANDLELIGHT REGENCY SPECIAL

Published by
Dell Publishing Co., Inc.
1 Dag Hammarskjold Plaza
New York, New York 10017

ISBN: 0-440-14617-8

Printed in the United States of America
Previous Dell Edition #4617
New Dell Edition
First printing—August 1978

CHAPTER 1

"Señorita Mara, the lord is here." Juana's gentle voice spoke to her in Spanish from the doorway of the bedroom.

Mara Pearsall gave a grimace of disgust. "He does not quit, that one," she said in reluctant admiration. "Very well, Juana. Serve him sherry. I will come down in a few minutes."

"Sí, señorita."

Juana withdrew and closed the door softly. Mara got up from her desk where she had been going over her father's papers. She crossed the bare shining parquet floors to the mirrored dresser and sat down on the heavy Spanish bench. She stared at herself with cool calculation.

The ugly, bulky black dress was good. It concealed her small petite figure, made her look plump and stooped. Deliberately she brushed out the long glossy blue-black hair curling below her shoulders and fastened it up into a bun at the back of her neck.

She studied herself again keenly. Then she added more of the graying powder which made her lightly tanned fresh complexion assume the sickly hue of a woman twice her years. She put on the thick black-rimmed spectacles she always kept ready and stood up to go. As a final gesture, she saluted herself sharply with a gamine grin, before she assumed the dark frowning look the waiting lord would recognize.

On her way down the hall she paused at an open door. Her vivid blue eyes, concealed by the dark spectacles, affectionately studied the stooped figure of the man at the desk.

"José, he is here again."

The tutor looked up from his desk, smiled to see her. His melancholy round face, his flashing brown eyes, his intelligent alert head, the quick-gesturing hands were as familiar to her as her own face and gestures.

"So? Be careful, Mara. Never underestimate the enemy. Better caution than betrayal."

"Sí, José. I understand." She gave him a quick curtsy, graceful in spite of her clumsy dress. He raised his hand in salute and again bent over the papers.

Thoughtfully Mara moved toward the dark stairway. All the house was in shadow, hushed as though in mourning for the master who had rarely graced it. It would have seemed a gloomy house for anyone unaccustomed to it. A single tall taper stood at the head of the stairs. Mara's hand reached for the railing, she placed her foot on the first step, started down soundlessly. As she moved, her skirts rustled stiffly.

A man stood at the foot of the stairs, staring at the portrait of her parents which had been hung twenty years before. Her tall dark father, his blue eyes smiling, the look of recklessness and impatience. Her small fragile brown-haired mother, unsophisticated curls framing the sweet, unawakened face.

The man turned and looked up at Mara as she descended the stairs. The single taper at the foot of the stairs flickered over his tall slim figure, highlighting the long, blond curly hair, the blue uniform and trim gold decorations, the cold blue eyes. His tanned, slender face and long nose seemed hawklike, hard. There were signs of dissipation in the lines under his eyes, the ruddiness of his cheeks. Sir Gaylord Humphrey, Viscount Kelton, had a reputation as a rake that exceeded his reputation as a fighter, which he had earned under Wellington.

"Three visits in three days. You do me too much honor, Lord Humphrey," said Mara frigidly, before she had reached him.

A gleam of grim humor lit the blue eyes. He reached gallantly for her hand. She permitted a light kiss sketched on the tips of her fingers, then attempted to withdraw her hand. His hold tightened. Unnecessarily he helped her down the last steps and turned her toward the formal drawing room.

"Oh, we have much to discuss, my ward," he said ironically, and bowed her into the room.

Her mouth tightened in a way that would have warned anyone who truly knew her, few as those persons were. The small round chin went up. She adjusted her annoying spectacles irritably and walked over toward the coffee tray.

"You have not been served sherry, my lord?" She frowned.

"I waited for you—my ward."

She seated herself, and after a pause he sat near her in a tall armchair of black leather. His blond head was thrown back, his blue eyes frankly studying her. She felt an unusual sense of unease, of danger.

She poured the rich Spanish sherry and handed the glass to him. For herself she poured the thick black coffee and added cream and sugar. Silently she offered biscuits, which were politely declined.

"Must you look like a middle-aged Spanish woman?" he blurted out abruptly, rudely. "If I did not know you for a British girl of two and twenty—"

She stiffened. A little bubble of laughter had all but escaped her. She primmed her mouth, drooped her eyelids.

"To dwell upon appearance is vanity, señor,"

she rebuked, as coldly as one of her nun-teachers could have done.

"My God," he groaned, and flung himself back in the hard unyielding high Spanish chair. He bent a darkly brooding look upon her. "Oh, well, something can be done, it must," he muttered.

She added to herself, "But not to me! I will not endure it!"

"When your father made me your guardian—" he began again.

"I was but a child, señor. Now, as you say, I am a female of twenty-two, and no guardianship is necessary."

"Nevertheless, I am your guardian until you marry. Until you *marry*, by God," he repeated, as though incredulous.

Now she did not have to pretend stiffness and fury. "You need have no concern for that, señor," she said sharply, in Spanish, then corrected herself and repeated in English. "I have no intention of marrying. I intend to devote myself to good works of charity and to literary studies. I have a devoted duenna. I shall live here quietly, in Madrid, and cause no scandal. There is no danger. Napoleon is defeated, the French have withdrawn—"

"You are an idiot! Spain is in a turmoil. The political situation could not be more uncertain," he told her sharply. "Hidden away in this dark tomb of a house, you can have no conception of what takes place in the outside world—"

"No, señor?" she asked, with assumed meekness, but again a naughty bubble of laughter wanted to well up inside her. If he only knew what she knew about the outside world—and how she had learned it, how horrified he would be! She and José had had more adventures in a few years than the gentleman languidly seated opposite her could have in a lifetime, she would warrant!

"Precisely. Well, let us not argue today," he said more calmly. "I have come on an errand of my sister, Mrs. Chandler. She is most eager to meet you."

I doubt that, flashed Mara's brain quickly. She refilled his glass of sherry as he continued.

"So I am commissioned to bring you to her. It is a warm sunny day. An outing will do you good," and he added a look of displeasure at her pallid face.

"Kindly convey my regrets to your sister," she began conventionally.

He held up his large tanned hand. "No, Mara! It will not do. My sister is inveterately curious, and her children are—" He grimaced. "My life is a torment," he complained, and a smile softened his hard mouth. "My sister Enid has added her two imps to my household, and they will not rest until they see the girl who has the misfortune to be Uncle Gaylord's ward!"

Now the laugh did bubble out and made him start. It was so youthful, so gay and excited. He sat upright with a jerk and stared at her.

"Oh—I beg pardon!" She sobered at once and drooped into her black dress, subsiding. "It did sound so—"

"You will come then? Good! You will need only a cloak, a shawl—" He stood up gracefully. He was like a tiger in his litheness, she thought involuntarily. He seemed so lazy and slow, then unexpectedly he would be on his feet, or a dozen yards away from where he had been. Deceptive strength, she analyzed.

"I did not mean—" she began.

He was looking at his watch. He returned it to its pocket, smiled down at her, so good-humoredly, so sympathetically, that she wanted to melt under his charm. "You will come and end this suspense? I cannot promise you an easy time, for they will shower you with a hundred questions— how you have lived in Madrid all this time of the Peninsular Wars, how you like Spain, Spanish food, clothing—" His eyes flickered at her dress, then politely away again. "Come! We shall be there in time for tea."

How he managed it, she did not afterwards understand. He flung a cloak about her, hustled her out to his waiting carriage, drove off with her before her breath could come twice. She flinched from the sunlight—surely he could see the gray powder on her face! But he did not notice, busily raising his hat a dozen times on the way to the smart section of Madrid where he lived.

She huddled beside him, resentfully aware of the smiles in his direction, the curious stares at herself, in the blue and gold carriage drawn by matched magnificent blacks.

"My home is called 'La Casa Dorada,'" he informed her breezily, on the way. "Ah, how do you do?" He bowed again to a smart Spanish lady and her ravishingly beautiful daughter. "Lovely women here," he commented to Mara. "Yes, Enid is my hostess, her husband is often absent on business. And her brats need a firm hand at times. She came down two months ago from England when I set up in Madrid."

He chatted on informally, ignoring her stiff silences, until they began to turn into an avenue of beautiful trees. In the distance she could see a golden house, bright in the sunshine, large and spacious and rambling. Beyond were the stables, and some magnificent grays and blacks were running loose in a pasture. She caught her breath at the beauty of the place as they approached.

"Lovely, eh? So many Spanish houses seemed so dark to me. I think they do it for the coolness. But I prefer the sunshine, and brightness and gaiety. When I saw this place, I took it at once. Look at the flowers—" She was looking, and could not keep from exclaiming at their beauty, to his satisfaction.

Flower beds lined the driveway as they came closer. They left the cool shade of the trees, and drove in sunlight, where carefully spaced pools and fountains were scattered among the areas of flowers. She had an impression of golden-orange, of reds and crimsons, of pinks and blues, and always the velvety green of the lawns between. The pools sparkled blue water, the fountains were of white stone in humorous shapes, little cupids, and fishes and dolphins and mythical animals. As they drove around the huge building to the side portico, she saw more gardens and pools extending into the distance.

"I thought perhaps you did not care for gardens, Mara," he finally commented, thoughtfully watching her face as she gazed and gazed.

"Oh—there has not been time," she said absently, then caught herself. "That is—the house took many hours. And I managed the household from the time I came here ten years ago. I was only twelve, but—Father was often gone—" In spite of her resolution to remain detached, her voice hardened and went cold at mention of her father.

"Yes, at the wars," he said, deliberately.

"His mistresses also took much time, my lord," she said frigidly, not looking at him. "He was often in southern Spain, or over in Italy, or back in England—once my mother was safely and conveniently dead!"

"Ah." He said only the monosyllable and then jumped down from the carriage. He reached up to help her down. She thought to take his hand, but he surprised her. He lifted her easily by her waist, his fingers sinking into the black bulky gown.

She stiffened in instant rage. "Put me down!" she ordered, and her blue eyes flashed fire.

"Of course, Mara," he said, and swung her out of the carriage, and to the ground beside him. There was a laugh line beside his mouth as she glared up at him, that and a surprised look. "You are much lighter than I would have thought!"

Her mouth tightened ominously. He ignored that and put his hand easily into her arm to lead her inside. He took her at once into a second-floor drawing room, where a lovely slim blonde woman sat beside a tea tray. She was wearing a blue muslin dress with blue silk ribbons, her hair dressed high. Only a look of dissatisfaction, of restlessness, marred her gracious appearance. She looked up at once as they entered, then moved to stand and came over to Mara.

"My dearest Mara, at last! I knew your father —I am so sorry to hear of his too early decease—" Her hands clasped Mara's warmly, the gentle blue eyes studying her.

"Thank you, Mrs. Chandler."

Sir Gaylord introduced them easily, informally, then swung around to the two children, who had left their seats near the fire and come forward curiously. "And these two brats here, straighten up young fellow!—this is Mistress Jennifer Chandler, known as Jennie, and her brother Fergus Chandler. Say hello nicely, and get back to your play!"

Jennie raised an eager blonde face to Mara's, curtsied solemnly, then burst out, "Oh, are you really defying Uncle Gaylord? That is so jolly! How do you do it?"

Mara gasped a little. Gaylord administered a light spank which did not deter her in the slightest. Jennie seemed as determined and charming as her uncle, quite set on having her questions answered.

Fergus was a dark, placid boy, who gave her a shy smile, then retreated to his cushion by the fire. He seemed more intent on consuming his cake than taking stock of the curiosity who was Mara.

Mrs. Chandler took Mara to sit beside her, gave her tea and cakes, and shushed Jennifer firmly. But the small girl sat down on a hassock at Mara's feet and studied her as intently as her uncle had done, making Mara feel a little uneasy.

After the usual polite inquiries, Enid Chandler said, "I am sure you will find the house quite charming, Mara. And if you desire other rooms than the ones you have been given, you have only to ask. I thought the quiet ones at the side, away from the children, would be best."

Mara started and met Gaylord's quiet gaze as he sat opposite them. "But I am not—" she began.

"You might give some advice to my sister concerning a Spanish tutor for the children," he interrupted casually. He crossed his legs and accepted another small cake from his sister.

She wrenched her mind from what his sister had said. Perhaps the woman did not understand she had refused to come and live with them. "A tutor? I do not know—" Then she thought of José. He could use the money. And he was not well. "I—I do know one man. The tutor I myself had," she said hesitantly. "He is not very strong. He is just recovering from an—illness." She dared not tell them it was a wound; they would ask too many questions. "But he is most intelligent, and speaks English, Spanish, and French fluently. His knowledge of history is wide—"

"Who is this paragon, and can he endure children such as mine?" asked Enid with eagerness and good humor.

"Why—I am sure he can. He is patient, gentle. And he has a fund of stories the children might like immensely."

"Stories! Oh, good," said Jennie, bouncing on the hassock at Mara's feet.

They asked his name, and she told them, "José Antonio y Moreno. He is of a good family, though they are poor now. He was well educated in the University. He is about thirty-five now, and—and most eager to please."

"Do send him to see me soon, darling," said Enid. "I am sure your recommendation will be sufficient for me! You have lived in Madrid about ten years, Gaylord says."

"That is correct. Since my mother died—in London. My father sent for me and insisted that I live with him. Though he was frequently away from home." Her gaze involuntarily met that of Gaylord, and she knew he was remembering her outburst about her father and his mistresses.

"Then you can tell me about the Madrid shops. I shall adore shopping with you. And those cunning cafés. Do you often go to the concerts?" Enid's blue gaze went absently to Mara's rusty, black bulky gown.

"I shop very little, Mrs. Chandler," said Mara stiffly. "I am absorbed in my studies. I am sure you will find more ladies who know about the shops—"

"But you will be here in the house. You can't shut yourself in all day," said Enid sunnily. "We can plan outings—that will amuse me—"

Mara compressed her mouth. "You do not understand, Mrs. Chandler! I do not intend to live here, no matter what your brother says! I have my own home to attend to, and my own life to live!"

"Oooooh," murmured Jennie, gazing up at her, with little hands clasped, and mischievous face alight. "You do explode, don't you, Miss Mara?"

Just then a footman came in and bowed to Mrs. Chandler. "The boxes of the Señorita Pearsall have all arrived and been placed in her rooms. Also the duenna has come and is unpacking. The rooms are ready, ma'am!"

Mara sprang to her feet, rage and shock bursting through her. "What? What? How dare you do this!" She swung on Gaylord as he politely stood also. "How dare you? I told you I would not live here! You may just pack them up and send them back! I have refused—"

"Gently, gently," he said, maddeningly calm, and a smile twitched the corner of his mouth. "You do remind me of your father more and more! You will like us when you come to know us, whether or not you think so now!"

"It is not a question of liking! Though I despise you! You are just like my father—a rake, a libertine—and I despise you as I hated him!" She yelled the words at him in a royal rage now, her fists clenched, her eyes flashing. "I give not a damn for his wishes! He is dead, and I shall live as I please!"

There was a short, shocked silence in the polite drawing room.

Then Gaylord said, "Mara, I will show you to your room. A little rest will do you and your temper some good! And I should warn you—I am quite strong. If you refuse to come, I shall carry you!"

"How dare you? You would not dare—"

He took a step toward her. She stood her ground, defying him, her head flung back. "You tempt me, dear," he said pleasantly, but coldly. "Do not make me use my strength against you! It would be quite useless. And if you think to run away—well, I shall find you and bring you back. I find your attitude toward your father quite shocking. I admired that man, and he happened to save my life several times. I shall carry out his wishes—to the last detail—because of that admiration and affectionate regard and keen sense of gratitude I feel toward his memory!"

"You are a bastard," she said. Enid squealed, but Mara's whole attention was on the man opposite her. "You cannot force me to marry—to do as *he* wished! I would rather be dead!"

"No doubt. But first you shall marry," he said. "Now, do you wish to be escorted to your rooms —or carried there by myself or the footman?"

He started toward her, and this time she turned and stalked from the room. She had never been so furiously enraged, so close to tears of sheer temper. She followed the footman up the stairs and down a long hallway to the east wing of the

Casa Dorada. There she found Juana and her boxes, in scattered confusion. The maid was quite shocked and in a flutter.

"Oh, Señorita Mara, what has happened to us? I thought you were determined not to come!"

Mara's mouth was set. "It shall not be long that we are here, Juana," she said grimly. "I think first we must endure some problems and straighten them out. There, there, do not tremble so! We shall settle all, in spite of that high lord!"

Juana was calmed and set to unpacking more black dresses, black mantillas, black shawls. She had also brought other boxes, and Mara was thankful she was unpacking for her, not a curious maid of the new household. For with the disguising dresses were other disguises—boys' garments, pants, and shirts, and caps—and her pistols and sword.

She picked up a pistol and weighed it thoughtfully in her hand. She probably would not need it again—but then again, she just might!

CHAPTER 2

Mara refused to dine with the family, sending a curt message that she was weary. A lavish tray was sent to her rooms, but she ate little. She turned over and over in her mind the ways she would use to escape the hated guardian and his ruling over her life.

At last she decided what she often did on her ventures—that she must wait and seize opportunity when it arose, as it frequently did. She went to bed early and rose early to go over her father's papers and some of her own, which fortunately had been brought from her own house.

Juana came to her at nine o'clock, surprised to find her up and dressed. "But why did you not ring for me, Señorita Mara? Don José has arrived and is with Mrs. Chandler. She seems pleased with our señor-tutor."

"Good, good. He moves fast, that one," Mara added absently, frowning as she did whenever she thought of Gaylord Humphrey. He was a high-handed one, but she could defeat him, as she had defeated others!

"And Mrs. Chandler sent the message she will be pleased for you to join them at breakfast, at your convenience."

Mara thought about it, then decided to do so. She must at least see José installed in his new post. And she must survey the grounds of the place, in case she wished to steal out at night, as she frequently did.

She dressed in the black gown, powdered her face more lightly, for daylight in this sunny open house was more revealing than her darkened house. She brushed out her long blue-black hair, then fastened it up in the huge bun which hung heavily on her slim neck.

"Ah, señorita, how I wish you would dress as other ladies do, in some pretty gown, which shows off your loveliness," sighed Juana unexpectedly. "How will you ever marry if no man sees how beautiful you truly are?"

Mara flung around in amazement. "You, too, Juana?" she asked. "You know how I feel about men! I hate them all."

"You do not hate Don José," said Juana wisely. "And others you worked with—some were good men. Someday you may wish to marry and have little ones of your own. But what man can see past—that?" And she pointed her finger at Mara's bulky gown.

"Really, Juana!" Mara frowned in displeasure. Juana had never talked like this before. The maid subsided, and Mara finished getting ready to be seen.

She went down to breakfast and entered the light sunny room with a feeling of unreality. This was truly a house of gold. Sunlight entered everywhere through the exuberantly opened French windows, billowing curtains, and reflected against white or lightly tinted walls. The breakfast room was radiant in pale blue and gold, with flowers in vases set about in a casual, yet effective, manner.

Gaylord rose at her entrance. Enid fluttered as she greeted Mara. "Good morning, dear Mara. I hope you slept well?"

"I hope she has regained her good temper," Gaylord teased, with a mocking smile.

Mara gave him a flashing glance from her vivid blue eyes and longed to slap his handsome face. "I slept well, thank you," she said coldly. Another man rose from beside Enid, a big older man, dark, ponderous. He must be at least ten years older than his wife, thought Mara, as Gaylord introduced his brother-in-law, Lyman Chandler.

"I thought we might go down to the shops today, Mara," said Enid Chandler brightly. "If you are rested—"

"I rarely go shopping, Mrs. Chandler," said Mara coldly. "As I informed you, there must be other ladies much more aware of fashion—"

Lyman Chandler looked thoughtfully at Mara's figure. "I should think you want to wear black for your father, my dear. But something a little smarter, more in fashion?"

"I have worn black for years," she forced herself to say quietly. "And I cared not a fig for my father! No, this is my preference!"

"Indeed," said Mr. Chandler, and addressed himself to his ham and eggs.

"May I remind you, Mara," said Gaylord, "that others might think your sentiments—or lack of sentiments—concerning your late father in rather bad taste? I would request that you keep your unfilial feelings to yourself!"

An ominous silence fell on the breakfast table. Enid finally broke it nervously by referring to José. She had been most impressed with him and wished to know further details about him. Mara informed her cautiously and managed to make polite conversation with her hostess until breakfast was ended.

Enid was visibly disappointed when Mara refused again to go shopping with her. But the project received another setback. A footman announced as they were leaving breakfast that a Mrs. Desmond had called and wanted to know if they were at home.

"But of course!" Enid brightened, then turned uneasily to Gaylord. "But—perhaps you have some appointment with her, dearest?"

"Not I. I was not aware that she rose so early in the morning," he said, with his detestably ironic smile. "Do let us greet her and find what causes her to be up and about so early."

"Oh, I expect she wants to meet Mara. I told her Miss Pearsall was coming to live with us." Enid flashed a mischievous look at Mara. "I expect she was worried—I mean—" And then she flushed red and looked guilty.

Mara said nothing, only followed her hostess with assumed meekness to the formal drawing room. This was done in deeper vivid blues and greens, touched with gold. More flowers were set in vases about the shining heavy Spanish tables. Enid—or someone—had succeeded in giving a lightness and airiness to an essentially Spanish house and furniture.

When they entered the drawing room, a woman sprang up to greet them. Mara stifled a gasp. The woman was tall and slim and had auburn hair and brilliant green eyes. She wore black, but a smart, shining black fabric in a dress cut to show the curves of her beautiful figure, setting off her creamy skin. She moved forward with the self-assured grace of a princess.

"Ah, Enid, I am so dreadfully early. But I had so much to accomplish today, and I had to come and see you first." The sharp green eyes went at once to Mara and seemed to burn through her.

The smile grew more pleasant. "So, this is the ward. Gaylord, you did not tell me she was older!"

"She is twenty-two, Vivienne, and don't be rude!" said Gaylord, with a laugh. He introduced them. "Mrs. Vivienne Desmond, Miss Mara Pearsall; her father, Brandon, was the son of my old friend Henry Pearsall, and then Brandon and I became friends as well. So I have known three generations of this family."

Ah, but you do not know me, thought Mara, her eyes narrowing.

She sat down demurely beside Enid on the plump sofa. Mrs. Desmond sat where she could see Mara and be near Gaylord, and by the way she kept turning to the viscount and demanding his opinion on this and his thoughts on that, Mara figured that was where the wind blew.

She was relieved when the woman left. Enid then departed on some shopping expedition alone, and Mara retired to her rooms. She was glad to throw off the heavy black dress, wash her face, and sit in a light negligee of white lace at her desk. The door was locked, and Juana stood guard as well, so she did not think she would be surprised.

But she felt uneasy here in this house. It was not like the dark shadowy house she was accustomed to. It was light, charming, bright, gay. There had been talk of balls and dinners, picnicking expeditions, visits, shopping, new dresses. It was all disturbing the reflection of her days, her plans for the future. Moreover, it was interrupting some important plans she had for helping the Spanish cause.

Mara found it difficult to concentrate on the papers today. She was anxious to get through her father's business correspondence and be finished with that. She could then forget the past and work on her own precious projects. She got up, wandered about the huge, airy room, peered out the barred Spanish grilled windows to the gardens. She studied the stables outside, the arrangement of flower beds and fountains, and for a time she longed to run free there, without her bulky dresses, in a little shift such as she had worn as a child. It seemed that she had not been a child since her mother had taken ill at their London home.

Her mouth drooped in heavy bitterness. Gaylord and the others did not comprehend her fury and hatred of her father. They did not know how he had deserted her mother and her, when her mother lay desperately ill for two years. Mara, at ten, had been in charge of the household. Her father did not even visit. And her mother had died deserted, bewildered, calling for the gay handsome man who had left her. Poor Anne Pearsall, the daughter of a country parson, married into an environment of such glittering sophistication she could not cope with it. She had not endured her husband's affairs silently. She had stormed, wept, wasted away. And he had left her.

And his daughter. The bitter girl had wanted to refuse to come to him at Madrid, but she had been too young to have a choice. She had come—but she had hated him silently, keeping the house too dark for his light spirits, keeping herself silent before him, obediently doing her lessons and managing the household silently, rejecting his few overtures, glad when he left Madrid, though she knew he went to be with one of his mistresses.

Gaylord was like him, she thought, and went back to her desk. She passed the huge mirrored dresser on the way and stopped to gaze at herself somberly. The white lace set off the peaches-and-cream complexion, the thick waves of blue-black curly hair, the slim rounded figure. But no man would see her like that, she vowed intensely, not for the first time. She hated men!

Mara sent her excuses for luncheon, and again a lavish tray was sent up. She ate and returned to work. Late in the afternoon Mrs. Desmond called again, and Mara received a message to come to tea. She refused through Juana. Enid Chandler came herself, but was turned away by Juana, who whispered that Señorita Mara was accustomed to taking a siesta during the afternoon.

"Oh—but I do hope she plans to come to dinner?" asked Enid anxiously. "Gaylord will be so furious if I don't get her to come—"

Mara grimaced to herself but prepared to go down to dinner later. She was deliberately long in coming, so that the time in the drawing room would be brief. She put on another of her black bulky gowns and powdered her face with gray. In addition to the heavy bun at her neck, she added a black shawl, some twenty years old, which had belonged to Juana. *That* should help convince them she did not belong in their society, she thought, with a gamine grin at herself in the mirror. She loved dressing in costume and deceiving everyone. It gave her a grim satisfaction that they could not see what she was really like.

She entered the drawing room quietly and was flustered when a dozen pairs of eyes turned to her. She had not dreamed there would be guests for dinner. She looked about rather wildly for a moment. Enid hastened to her side.

"Dear, are you rested? Do come and meet everyone." And the kindly woman took her hand. She began to introduce her, first to the ladies, of whom Mara knew several. Mrs. Desmond was there, radiant in emerald silk, the color of her eyes.

"And this is—our dear Mara Pearsall. Mara, darling, this is Señor Sanchez-Garcia." At Enid's gay voice Mara looked up, and a grim cold fear spread through her. She met the cold black eyes, saw the slick black hair, the small slick black mustache—

"Señor," she whispered. "Yes—we have met."

Gaylord was standing near them. She could not show emotion. She braced herself. She would not touch this man's hand; she would not allow him to kiss her fingers!

He did not reach out, and she backed slightly away.

"Señorita Pearsall. Yes, we have met. How do you do? My condolences on the death of your famous father," said the cold remembered voice, and he bowed slightly.

"Gracias, señor," she answered automatically in Spanish. "You are most kind to—to remember—" She turned blindly away, the shock running through her in tingling warning waves.

Lope Sanchez-Garcia. So he was back in Madrid, and in society again! She must tell José as soon as possible. And Sanchez-Garcia knew her, knew where she was. He had seen her face that horrible night, when her little guerrilla band had unmasked his younger brother Cristobal and— and—

She shuddered, then felt a hand take her heavy black shawl from her and set it more closely about her shoulders.

"You are cold, Mara?" The gentleness in Gaylord's voice shocked her anew. She stared up at him wildly. He frowned slightly, would have spoken, but Mrs. Desmond laid her jeweled white hand lightly on his arm and attracted his attention.

Mara was numb. That this one should have returned, as though nothing had happened! What was Spain today that it should be allowed! It spoke well for the chaos of its political situation that men like Lope Sanchez-Garcia walked freely in its streets and were received in the drawing room of an English viscount!

They went in to dinner, and she sat silently, between two Spaniards, not attempting to make any conversation until she felt a little more recovered. Then she turned to one . . . and they spoke of horses and the religious fete soon to take place.

"Señorita Pearsall, you speak Spanish so beautifully. Have you lived in Madrid all your life?" The British gentleman across from her leaned forward with a kindly smile.

The cold clear voice of Lope Sanchez-Garcia spoke up, and she shuddered again. "She has lived here some ten years, I believe. She and my younger brother Cristobal were once close friends—no? Unfortunately my brother died in the late war. A true tragedy from which I shall never recover. So young, so full of promise, yes, señorita?"

She forced herself to look into the glittering black eyes and murmur something conventional.

He was threatening her, he told her silently; he held her fate in his cruel hands. And that he would be harsh with her, she had no doubt.

"I thought Spanish men and women did not know each other," said Mrs. Desmond lightly. "Do enlighten me, someone? How could Miss Pearsall come to know a young Spanish man? Was she allowed more freedom than most Spanish girls—and most English girls?" Her gaze flicked contemptuously on Mara's dress and hair and face.

Mara did not answer, as though unaware she was being challenged. She felt a deep contempt for the woman. She knew her reputation. She had married an elderly man, a Britisher, and now she was a rather wealthy widow. Her kind haunted society, in London and in Madrid. Parasites, thought Mara, and turned her shoulder.

The lightly malicious gossip began to flow about her. She had heard such talk at her father's table—but she had refused to be hostess for him. She had heard the talk from the pantry where she had supervised the bringing of hot dishes to the table, the preparation of the cold sweets and the wines, and coffee. She had not been in a situation where she had been forced to participate in it.

"And do you now study at something?" persisted the young Englishman across from her.

"I am pursuing some studies of my own, comparing Cervantes and Shakespeare," she said deliberately, clearly. "It is a study which will cover both the ideology and the grammatical constructions which have fascinated me." And she went on in this way, until his bored set face finally turned from her back to his partner.

Later in the hallway Gaylord caught her by a shoulder and swung her around. He was scowling. "I invite a fine young man to meet you, and you bore him with talk of literary matters! And you dress like that! What am I going to do with you?"

"You will learn to let me alone," she said frigidly.

"Oh, no! You are going to meet young men, you are going to dress better, and that hair—by God, you are going to do something with that! And I'll take you riding and get some color in your face—"

He halted abruptly. Lope Sanchez-Garcia was brushing past them in the hallway, deliberately listening. Mara felt the same cold chill come over her. She must find José—but he could not help her much. His health was weakened by the infection that had long surrounded the bullet wound. He was no longer strong. But she felt in grave danger.

She shook off Gaylord's hand and said brusquely that she was retiring. He made no attempt to keep her, glaring after her as she mounted the stairs.

While the guests chattered in the drawing rooms and later played cards and drank wine and laughed, she and José talked in hushed tones in his drawing room. She was relieved to find that he had been treated courteously, given a suite of rooms on the fourth floor near the schoolroom, and was comfortable. They discussed the potential danger of the return of their old enemy, then their talk wandered to Mara's position in this household. José was worried for her and warned her that Gaylord was devious and might plan sudden moves to force her into marriage. "He takes his responsibilities seriously, little Mara! Even the children know he plans to marry you off soon and fulfill his obligation to your father."

"He will not succeed in that. I shall run away first," she declared firmly.

"Have a care," warned José. "Be on your guard. He is a man of more depth than one might suspect!"

It was late when she left his drawing room and crept in her heelless Spanish slippers down the servants' steps to the third floor. She was walking soundlessly along the darkened hallway toward her room when she heard voices, and a door opened near her.

She crouched against the wall, behind a heavy Spanish chest, and listened.

Gaylord was coming out of his sister's room. "Well, not impossible, Enid!" he was drawling.

"She is going to be a chore to marry off—by God, that shape! That face! One point in her favor though, she does have a pretty voice."

"And a temper, Gaylord! Don't forget that! If she is determined not to marry—"

"She is not as strong-willed as I am! We shall see, Enid! Goodnight!" And he went off down the hall toward the other wing, whistling under his breath.

Behind his back, Mara stuck out her tongue at him.

CHAPTER 3

The next two days Mara stuck to her rooms. She pleaded weariness, the pressure of working on her father's papers, any excuse she could think of. She thought they would tire of her, and let her go home.

Instead, her guardian came to her. Juana warned her, and Mara fled to her bedroom and hastily donned the heavy black dress, while Gaylord cooled his heels in her drawing room.

She powdered heavily, and when she came out her head was dropping meekly, her face looked drawn with fatigue. She knew the art of make-up, and a few lines near the eyes and mouth drawn with a pencil could do the trick.

He stared at her with a frown, but said in a rather gentle voice, "Mara, I am sorry you are so fatigued."

"Thank you, señor," she said, her mouth prim. She gave a little sigh, deliberately. "There is so much to be done. My father was not an orderly person. I think I ought to return to the house to work."

"And I am not Señor. My name is Gaylord. I give you leave to use it," and he gave her a mocking bow, his dark blue eyes twinkling. She stared down at the tips of her heavy shoes.

"So, Mara. I have decided that you ought to go out more. To stay in the house continually cannot be good for you. We are going out in the carriage this morning."

She started. "We—but, señor—I have much to do—"

"You will do a better job of it for some airing. Come, where is your cloak? The morning air has a decided chill to it, but it should put some color in your cheeks. And I have something serious to discuss with you, also, child."

She scowled. "I am not a child!" she fired, forgetting her meekness.

"Good, then I shall speak to you as one adult to another," he said calmly. "Your cloak—thank you, Juana." And he flung the cloak about her, took her arm forceably and led her from the room. She stared back helplessly at Juana, who smiled—a satisfied little smile which Mara did not like!

The October air was brisk and chilly, but invigorating. She drew great breaths of it, once the carriage was under way. It was such a smart spanking carriage of blue and gold, and the matched blacks set out at a fine pace. She would have enjoyed it if it had not been for the man who sat beside her.

He did not try to irritate or anger her, though. He spoke little, only to inquire if she were warm enough, if her seat was comfortable. She murmured her responses and sat alertly gazing about her. She adored Madrid, now coming to life following the devastation of the wars. The houses seemed brighter in the sunlight, people's faces wore smiles, there was a lilt to the very air and the birds' songs.

She was startled when the carriage drew to a halt in the center of fashionable Madrid, in front of a shop. She looked about as Gaylord jumped down and reached up for her.

"Where are we—oh!" she said, and sat flatly in her place, glaring down at him. "I will not go to a dressmaker's!"

"Señora Rodriguez is very clever with clothes. I only want you to look at some models she has ready," he said calmly. "Come, Mara! If you do not get down by yourself, I shall carry you in!"

There was a devil in his bright eyes, and a set to his chin that warned her. "Oh—you—you—you devil!" she sputtered. He reached up for her and picked her up bodily by the waist and set her down on the walk outside the shop.

"Coming in?" he inquired casually, and put his hands on her waist again. "Or shall I carry you?" he added silkily.

She tossed her head and walked inside the shop. She would not have been a female if she had not been entranced at once. The shop of Señora Rodriguez was one of the best in Madrid, and it was full of the most beautiful gowns Mara had ever seen outside a ballroom. White muslins, white silks, chiffons, blue velvets, crimson silks, and brocades—she gazed from one to the other, until she saw the middle-aged Spanish lady coming toward them.

Señora Rodriguez was plump, with an alert walk, snapping black eyes, and a charming smile for the British gentleman and his ward.

"Lord Humphrey," she murmured in English. "A pleasure, sir! I have an assortment of dresses for you to inspect. If the lady will accompany me—?"

Mara bit her lips, glanced at the lord. His eyes warned her. She tossed her head and followed the señora to a back fitting room. There the rusty black cloak and gown were removed, and the señora stared at her in visible wonder.

"But you—you are much smaller than I had imagined—" she murmured. She snapped her fingers and gave orders in Spanish, rapidly, and the little maids went scurrying. A blue silk gown was brought, Mara's glasses were removed before she could protest, the silk gown was slid onto her slim rounded form, and she was whirled to the large mirror.

"There, my little señorita, what do you think of yourself?" asked Señora Rodriguez in great excitement. "What a wonder! But the powder on your face—all wrong—" And she wiped at it with a cloth. In a few movements she unbound the thick ugly bun and let the blue-black hair sweep down. "A few curls at the shoulder, and—ah!"

Mara stared and stared. She herself could not have imagined such a transformation. In the mirror her image stared back at her in blue-eyed wonder. The slim petite form in the clinging blue silk gown, the low neck revealing the creamy skin, the mussed blue-black curls floating about her neck and shoulders, the sparkle in her eyes as she stared—She was beautiful! She, Mara, was beautiful!

Then she remembered. "No, no, no, I cannot wear this! Give me my black dress again! No, no, I shall not—" she said, and snatched at the black gown wildly.

"But señorita," cried Señora Rodriguez. "It is perfect—you are beautiful—men must see you like this—what a shame—oh, no, you must not change—oh, señorita—"

"I will not wear it! No, take it off, and give me back my spectacles!" Mara held the black gown in front of herself defensively, almost crying in her anxiety. No one must see her like this. She must have been mad to come in here at all!

"What is this?" Sir Gaylord Humphrey flung

back the curtains of the dressing room and strode inside unceremoniously. "What is going on? Why the argument—ah! ahhhh!"

He stared at Mara, then took the black rusty gown from her nerveless grasp and flung it to the floor. He stared at her, up and down, until she cringed, and her cheeks flooded red with color.

"You—little—minx! You devil! You did that deliberately!" he charged, his blue eyes flashing. "You dressed like that—and you could look—you devil! You were fooling us all! I should shake you!"

He reached out for her, and she thought he was going to carry out his threat. Instead, his hand flipped at the blue-black curly hair; his big fingers smoothed out a long curl to lay it on her creamy shoulder.

"Mara! I'll be—damned!" he said. Deliberately he took the rusty black gown in his hands and ripped it. She cried out in outrage.

"You let that alone! I will not wear these clothes. Give me back my dress—oh, my spectacles!" She screamed, for he had knocked the spectacles to the floor, and deliberately he crunched them underfoot, his boot grinding the glass into the rug, before the fascinated gaze of Señora and her little maids.

"I don't know what your little game was, but it is over, dear ward," he said grimly.

She flew at him and beat her fists impotently against his chest. He caught at the fists and held them tightly, staring down at her. "How dare you —how dare you!" she screamed, all restraints gone. "I will not obey you! You are the devil. You cannot force me to do what I will not!"

"You are my ward—until you marry. And with your looks—your figure—and your money, my dear!—you shall marry, and marry well! I'll see to that," and he nodded in satisfaction, his mouth hard and set.

"I will not! I hate men! I hated my father, I hated him for the way he treated my mother! I will never marry! I will never subject myself to the treatment—I will not marry! *Jamás! Jamás!*" she screamed in Spanish hysterically, pounding her free fist at his chest as he let her go for a moment.

"*Jamás*—never. Oh, yes, I think so, Mara." He held her roughly for a moment, making her feel his strength. Then he seemed to soften, his voice calmed. "Listen to me, my dear. Listen to me! Listen!"

He half-shook her, but his voice had gentled. She stared up at him, her wide blue eyes brimming with tears of anger.

"Listen, my dear," he said soothingly. "Listen. Will you listen?"

"No!" she blurted, and he shook her again.

"Yes, you will. You cannot live in the past. That is over, finished. Forget all that. Live in the present, plan for the future. Your future can be glorious, beautiful, as your past was stifled and bitter. Do you believe that?"

"No!" she said again, and stormed it at him. "No, no, no, I will not listen to you!"

"Yes, you will," he said quietly. "You will forget the past. You will wear beautiful clothes, you will dance and flirt and enjoy the friendship of men—yes, you will!" he repeated as she shook her head so violently her dark hair flew about his hands as they held her shoulders tightly. "You will some day come to love, yes, even you, Mara! You will love, and want to marry, and if the man is right for you, I shall approve! And you shall marry and have children—and treat them better than your parents treated you. Yes? Would you not like that?" His voice had softened marvelously as he gazed down steadily at her face.

"No, I do not wish it!" she said, but the fire had gone out of her, leaving her limp from her fury. "No, I wish to be left with my studies and my work—"

"You will change your mind," he told her arrogantly, and turned to the Señora Rodriguez, who had been a fascinated spectator at the scene. "Señora, please—you will bring out the loveliest ball gowns, the silks and satins and taffetas—"

"And the chiffons and muslins," sighed the señora, with her plump hands at her bosom. "Such a lovely charming girl—so soft and silky—she should be dressed in the softest fabrics, the most feminine—"

"No, no!" said Mara, but they no longer paid any attention to her. Sir Gaylord left the dressing room briefly, while they tried on gown after gown; then he would return to approve or disapprove. She stood for two hours, while white muslins and pink silks, and blue satins, and white chiffons, and dress after dress after ballgown after ballgown, and coats and cloaks and bonnets and gloves were brought for his inspection and approval.

When they finally left the shop, Mara was wearing the first blue silk dress, a fine white cloak, and a white bonnet with deep blue ribbons which matched her eyes, long white gloves, smart white silk slippers. She had tried to fasten her hair up into a bun, but it was sternly forbidden by her guardian. And her spectacles had been swept up by a little maid and flung into a dust bin.

Once back at La Casa Dorada, Gaylord insisted on showing off Mara to his sister. Enid exclaimed, offered tea, chatted charmingly to her, while little Jennie sat at her feet and stared up at her. The small girl finally said solemnly, "I like you much better this way. But you will not be fashionable, will you, and hateful, and hard?"

"My God," said Enid helplessly, and Gaylord burst into laughter, lounging in a deep but comfortable Spanish armchair.

"I intend to return to my old self," said Mara, nodding her head decidedly. But she had forgotten her flyaway hair, and it blew about her shoulders, and she brushed it back impatiently.

"No, you shall not go back, there is no return for you, my dear," said Gaylord. "And tomorrow night, at the ball, Enid, she shall wear a gown of white chiffon caught up with red roses, and all Madrid shall fall at the feet of the beautiful charming heiress."

"Do stress the word heiress," said Mara caustically, her mouth tight, her small round chin held high. "I am sure the men will come running then! They will be most devoted—until I marry one. And he will be devoted—until the knot is securely tied! Then watch him chase after the next girl he wishes—and return to his mistresses! Ah, yes, I know society well! They all act alike!"

Jennie cupped her small chin in her hands, drinking it all in avidly. Even little Fergus stopped his contented playing to gaze up at her seriously. Enid frowned and blushed a little unexpectedly.

"I am sure, dear, you are too hard on—society," she began, fumbling with her teacup.

"Mara, I do not want you to talk like this," Gaylord said sternly. "And do not frighten off the men, or I shall be angry with you! Enid, why don't you go upstairs with Mara and let her try on the white chiffon dress for you? You might advise her about a hairstyle—perhaps with curls piled high, a red rose in her hair."

He got up abruptly and left the room. Enid sighed and went with Mara to her rooms. Mara stormed into the room, glared at the piles of boxes from which Juana was unpacking dress after cloak after bonnet—and went over to her open closets. Then she stared.

"My black dresses, where are they?" she yelled. "Juana! Where are my dresses?"

"Ah—the lord ordered them burned, Señorita Mara," said Juana, her bright black eyes shining. "He ordered new dresses for you—see how pretty!"

Mara let out a cry of pure rage, and Enid ran from the room. Juana withstood the storm sturdily, finally placating her furious mistress with the promise that she would obtain one black dress for her—if she could. But Mara realized that her usually loyal maid and duenna had defected to the enemy, and she retired to her bedroom to rage by herself.

At least her secret horde of boys' clothing was still there, but she could not wear that as a usual disguise, she thought angrily.

Again she remained in her rooms, refusing to come out for luncheon or dinner. Enid came to plead with her, but she turned a deaf ear. Even little Jennie came pattering in to talk to her and tell her how pretty she was now. "Why don't you want to be pretty, Auntie Mara?" she asked innocently, her eyes curious.

Mara would not stir out, until Sir Gaylord came to her the next day.

"Now, Mara, no more stubbornness," he said firmly. "You will dress for the ball this evening. It is my first large splash here in Madrid; Enid has taken a great deal of trouble with it, and it is your debut! You will come—and you will wear the white chiffon dress I ordered for you—and you will behave yourself!"

He glared at her. She glared back defiantly. "And if I will not?" she said coldly.

"I will come up here, and I will carry you down to the ballroom, dressed in a nightshift, if you please! But you shall attend that ball, and you shall behave as I tell you! Or I shall also spank you as you should have been spanked years ago!"

"You are a bully, a rake, a libertine, a bastard," she said furiously, and clenched her fists. "You are worse than my father! At least he left me alone to do as I wished!" She added more curses in Spanish, deliberately trying to infuriate him. If he struck her, she would kill him!

He only smiled, infuriatingly, with that set cold look to his face. "Call me what you will in private, in Spanish or English, my dear! But in public, you will be polite, you will be charming to my sister, you will be gracious, and you will be well-dressed!" And he left her bedroom abruptly.

She stormed to herself and went to José, who only shook his head. His gaze lingered on her slim petite figure in the white muslin, the blue ribbons tied high under her soft rounded breasts.

"Mara, Mara, it was inevitable," he said gently. "You are a woman, a very attractive lady. What else will become of you? You could not hide yourself forever."

"Yes, I could. Yes, I could!" And she stormed away from him angrily. She had thought her old friend would understand.

She went down to the ball finally, dressed in white chiffon, the wide skirts dotted with tiny red rosebuds, her hands hidden in long white silk gloves. But her hair was tied up in the ugly bun and her face was gray with heavy layers of powder. Men glanced at her, sighed, offered to dance. She would accept, only to stumble deliberately with them, rejoicing in the pained expressions as they turned away after one brief dance. She was back in a corner, glaring at men, when someone came up beside her. She scowled—then turned rigid with fright.

Lope Sanchez-Garcia stood beside her. His plump heavy body was forced into a grand uniform of the Spanish colors. His black hair was pasted down, his black eyes glittered. She rememberd how he had looked that night, in ropes, straining against them as sentence was pronounced against his young brother.

"Ah, Señorita Pearsall, the lovely heiress," he said with a set smile. "This is your evening of triumph, is it not?" His black eyes flickered over her hair, her face, then deliberately down over her white-clad figure. She shrank from him, and his smile deepened. "How well I remember my young brother, Cristobal, at twenty-two. That was the year of his death, you recall. One never knows how short life can be, eh?"

"That is correct, señor," she said frigidly, regaining her composure. Her nerves tingled, she felt alive and aware, the way danger always affected her. "And when a traitor is discovered, it can be short indeed! One is never too young to betray, eh?"

They were speaking rapidly in Spanish. His smile altered to a set grimace. "I do not forget anything, señorita," he reminded her swiftly, as Sir Gaylord came over toward them. "Remember —you recall—twenty-two—the year of surprises! Enjoy yourself, señorita!" he said in English, smiled, bowed, as Gaylord came up to them.

Gaylord caught at Mara's wrist as she would have turned from him. "No, come with me!" he said grimly, and led her toward the French windows, where the ballroom overlooked the gardens. On the way, Mara caught a glimpse of Enid Chandler, looking unusually flushed and beautiful and starry-eyed. She was dancing in the arms of the young Spanish guardsman who was assigned to their protection.

Ramón Olivera was a most attractive young man. But why was Enid Chandler looking like that at him—as though she could not tear her gaze from his face?

Then Mara forgot Enid and stumbled as Gaylord dragged her down the steps. "Wait—wait—my shoe!" she gasped, as the unaccustomed white satin slipper fell off.

He stopped, knelt, picked up the shoe and set it on her foot. Her flesh seemed to tingle where he touched it briefly. Then he was on his feet again, dragging her with him. He went over to the nearest fountain, still pulling her along. He freed one hand and took out his white handkerchief. He dipped it into the fountain, and before she knew what he was about, she had a face full of water.

"Oh—you—what—what—" she sputtered wildly. He washed her face mercilessly, with a hard hand and a dripping kerchief, until she felt the skin was almost scrubbed off.

Then a swift hand went to the pins of her ugly bun. He ripped out the pins so hard that he pulled at her hair. When the pins had fallen to the ground, he yanked at her hair and pulled it all down, spreading it over her bare shoulders. She glared up at him, stunned and infuriated.

"Now, Mara, if you ever again dare to wear that infuriating bun—if you ever again put on gray powder—I shall spank you! Is that understood? How dare you defy me? I am very angry with you. Several gentlemen have informed me that you danced very poorly, that you talked Latin and Spanish to them, that you scared them off with talk of Cervantes and Shakespeare and what not! How dare you? You know my motives, I mean to marry you off. How can I do this, if you—"

"Exactly, and I will not obey you!" she cried out, her head flung back, her slim back proudly erect. "You know my feelings! I shall not marry! You cannot force me to marry one of them! I shall not! *Jamás, jamás!*"

"Never is a long time, my dear," he said grimly. He bent down, and she thought he would shake her or spank her. Instead, he pulled her recklessly into his arms, so that her whole slim body fell against his hardness. He ducked down, and his lips brushed against her flushed wet cheek.

She felt wild emotions such as she had never felt before. She thought she had hated when Cristobal Sanchez-Garcia had betrayed them, and she herself had directed the verdict of death. She had thought she hated when a gang had attacked them and shot José—and she had shot two of the gang, killing one of them. But never had she felt such wild emotions as raged through her now. She was being held tightly, a kiss pressed to her face, the hateful contact of his warm body against hers —a man who continually forced her to do what she would not, a man, a rake whom she despised, whom she hated as she had hated her father, forcing her to endure—

She pushed him back from her with a shaking hand, glaring up at him in the moonlight. "I hate you—I hate you—I hate you—" she hissed in Spanish. "I will never forgive you—"

"Go inside," he said curtly, angrily. "I will speak to you tomorrow! We shall reach an understanding! Go!" And he turned her and pushed her toward the lighted windows.

She raced away from him, but not toward the music of the ballroom. Instead she reached the edge of the veranda, then turned and ran toward the back of the huge house. She took refuge in some bushes, gasping for breath, full of such heated anger that she could not think clearly. Finally she began to recover her breath.

When she heard footsteps on the long veranda, she shrank back further into the bushes, hating the white fluffy dress that might betray her. Then she heard the husky voices and smiled in contempt. These were lovers, they would pay no attention.

"Ramón—Ramón—" moaned a woman's familiar voice. Shocked, Mara peered out to see the white arm of the lady reach up and pull down the head of the handsome guardsman.

Ramón Olivera—and Enid. The young bache-lor and the older married woman! Mara stood still, holding her breath, feeling both contempt and pity. Enid, married to a man years her senior, feeling trapped, with discontent and wistfulness written on her face—she must have fallen easy prey to the charm of the handsome Spaniard.

Mara stood still, uncomfortably quiet, while they kissed and whispered to each other, until they finally left and walked slowly back to the ball.

Finally she turned and ran into the house by the back hall and up to her room. She had had enough of society for tonight—forever!

CHAPTER 4

More clothes arrived, boxes stamped with the signature of Señora Rodriguez, other boxes with the marks of a famous bootier, gloves from another source, fans, mantillas of the most fragile white and black lace.

Worst of all—the riding habit. Juana removed it from its paper wrappings, held it up, murmured over it lovingly. It was blue velvet, shining and beautiful, flowing in wide skirts from a narrow waist. With it, gloves, boots, and the crowning touch—a tall hat of blue with shining blue plumes.

"Ah, Señorita Mara, look at this loveliness! What a sight for the young men of Madrid you will be! How everyone will stare and gaze at my señorita! Ah, you will be such a beauty!"

"Not I. Put it away, Juana! I mean it—I will not wear it! How dare he order those—those things for me! The impudence! Does he think he can force me to obey his will, when I would not yield to my father's? I am a woman—he cannot force me to do anything at all!" And Mara stamped her small foot and fled to consult José.

José had released the children from their studies and was seated at the desk in the small nicely furnished schoolroom. She was pleased to see the bright fire in the fireplace, to realize he was warm and comfortable, and from his face, seemed contented.

He lifted his head from the school books when she entered. He smiled his gentle calm smile. He was always in such control, she thought affectionately.

"Ah, come in, Mara. I do not see much of you, but you are busy, yes, and happy?"

She grimaced. "Busy, but not happy," she said, and her injuries returned to plague her. "Listen, José, he means to marry me off! I shall have to return to the house, or perhaps go to the country—"

"Do not rush into decisions, Mara. Think, wait, plan. Outguess the enemy," he advised placidly. "He cannot drag you to a priest and force you to say your responses. Think, girl. You can do only what you wish. So? Do not let him infuriate you. You do not think best when you are angry."

She sighed and sat down at the small school desk before him, feeling a child again in front of her tutor. "Always you are the sensible one," she said, feeling at ease in the usual Spanish. "But I am worried also, José," and she switched back to English, as they often did, back and forth, to give them both practice.

"What is the trouble, Mara?"

"It is Lope Sanchez-Garcia. He was at the ball last night. He threatened me. You know, I cannot comprehend why the society has allowed him to return! He betrayed us to Napoleon's troops, he is a traitor. Yet—"

"But the king returned also."

"The people do not understand."

"No, the politics are confused. Ah—well—we must help plan and perhaps later—but Lope Sanchez-Garcia. His threats. What did he say?"

She told José briefly, and he sat with his head in his palm. "So—he means to revenge the death of young Cristobal. That worthless dog," he added with contempt. "Always so greedy for money—he took the gold and sold us. You did right to order his death. That does not worry you, does it? The regrets?"

"No regrets! I would do it again! I would shoot him myself, rather than order it done!" she said spiritedly, though with a shudder. The boy had died hard. "Ah, God, wars are hard! Shall we be done with them now, José?"

"God knows it, not I, little one. And the other deaths, you do not regret shooting—"

"Never! They had shot at you, my friend, my only friend and compadre! And that wound still plagues you! If I could change history, that is what I would change—that you should not have been shot—"

"Where were you shot, señor?" The shrill piping voice broke in on their low-toned conversation, and the two of them sat turned to stone, as the bright faces of Jennie and Fergus peered into the room from the bedroom beyond. It was Fergus who had piped up.

Jennie led him into the schoolroom, seeing that they were discovered. "Fergus doesn't make a good spy," she said brightly. "He won't be quiet!"

The dark-haired boy grinned and repeated his question, "Where were you shot, Señor Antonio?"

José and Mara were exchanging horrified glances, but José, never upset for long, took the situation in hand. "I will tell you, but you must solemnly promise not to betray us!"

Jennie's blue eyes and Fergus's dark ones glistened with excitement and pleasure. "I promise," said Fergus at once.

"I will if you tell me some more," said Jennie. "Who did Mara shoot?"

Mara swallowed and drew the light white shawl more closely about herself. "How much did you hear, Jennie?" she asked, with forced quiet.

"Oh, I heard you say that the horrid señor longname has threatened you, and it's because of his brother Cristobal—what an odd name!"

José took over once more. "If others hear about

this, little Mara will be in grave danger of her life, and I also," he said impressively. "Do you swear, Jennie, that you will not tell about this? Then I will show you my wound."

Jennie was unable to resist. "I swear," she said eagerly. "Oh, I do swear! I will not cause Mara any trouble, truly I will not. I swear to keep silent about her shooting Cristobal!"

José impressively had them swear on the Bible nearby, and Mara bit her lips to keep back a bubble of laughter as the two children took their oaths. Then José drew open his shirt and showed them the bandage, and cautiously opened it a little to show the angry red wound still festering. It was both impressive and sickening, and the children's curiosity was quite satisfied.

Jennie and Fergus accompanied Mara back to her rooms, the little girl hanging onto Mara's hand and chattering happily. "I do love your new dresses, Mara," she was saying, as they entered Mara's sitting room.

Mara halted abruptly. Gaylord was seated on the edge of one of her chairs, his face set grimly. His face softened a little as she entered with the children. He stared at her, as he rose to his feet.

"Where have you been, Mara?"

"With the children," she said coldly. "Is it your concern?"

"We have guests this morning. I have been looking for you to come to the drawing room. I wished to make sure you were properly dressed. Run along, little ones! You might get some cakes if you hide in a corner of the room and pretend you aren't there!"

Both children shrieked with glee and ran away, racing down the hallway. Gaylord looked over Mara critically, and she shrank from his cool look at her white dress with the purple ribbons. Her hair streamed loose. Juana had come in quietly from the bedroom.

"A matching purple ribbon for her hair, Juana, tie it back gracefully. Or bring the ribbon to me—"

"I can dress myself, thank you," said Mara, furiously. "If you will kindly leave me—"

"We have waited long enough! I will escort you down. Ah, thank you." He took the purple ribbon from Juana, sat Mara down in a chair before she knew what he was doing, threaded the ribbon through her dark hair, and tied it flat on top of her head. Juana, with hands clasped, obviously admired his work. Mara could have slapped her.

"If you are quite done, señor—" She started to rise. He helped her up, unnecessarily, and stared at her face critically.

"No gray powder? Good. You could use a little rouge—no, there is some color in your cheeks, from anger, no doubt," he said ironically, that twisted smile at the corner of his mouth. "Ah—Mara, how long have you known Señor Lope Sanchez-Garcia?"

She started visibly and clasped her cold hands together. He was studying her narrowly. "Why—he—they were friends of my father, in the old days, señor. They came to the house. But I did not know them very well. Not very well at all."

"He said you played with his brother Cristobal."

"We might have played in the gardens a few times—but I did not play much, señor. I was twelve, thirteen, fourteen. I began to run the household and was much occupied." She braved his look.

He took her arm, and they began to leave the room. "I should warn you, Mara," he said in a low tone, so Juana could not hear. "There is some gossip around Madrid. Mrs. Desmond was good enough to warn me this morning; she is in the drawing room now. Señor Sanchez-Garcia says there is some talk about you and a—well, a lover."

"A lover!" Mara stopped dead in her tracks and glared up at him. "A lover! Are they insane? I would never—never—I hate men!"

"So you have informed me," he said drily. "Come along! I shall quell the gossip as best I can. I merely wondered if the lover could have been Cristobal."

"I despised him!" she told him angrily. "He was a weakling, a traitor, a stupid little greedy—" She stopped abruptly.

"That does not sound like love, to be sure," he

said more lightly. "Ah—here we are. Compose your face, please, Mara! You reveal too much sometimes. Your eyes are most expressive. No wonder you covered them with those dreadful spectacles!"

They walked into the drawing room, and Mara tried hard to compose her face. She was aware of Mrs. Desmond's hard gaze on her, the jealous, infuriated, baffled look of a woman who has underestimated an enemy.

Mara went over to sit beside Enid. She was quite aware of the bright demure face of Jennie, as the child sat on a hassock close enough to hear the gossping of the adults, and absorb it all. Mara was aware of some danger in the situation. Could Jennie and Fergus be trusted to remain quiet, with such a lovely assorment of dangerous morsels to reveal? Fergus was munching away at a tea cake in his corner, quite satisfied to play there so long as he was well fed.

Secrets, secrets. Some bloody and dreadful, some sordid and pathetic. Enid sitting beside her, bright-eyed for once, with bloom in her cheeks, probably thinking of the handsome Spanish guardsman.

Mrs. Vivienne Desmond was sitting near Gaylord and playing with her rings nervously. They were beautiful huge stones, of diamonds and emeralds. Why was she back here in Madrid so soon after the wars? Mara did not wonder for long. She was following Gaylord, she thought wisely, noting the woman's fond looks at the man. Love, or desire. What a dreadful thing it did to people, like Enid and Mrs. Desmond. It made them lose their pride, their dignity, their self-respect, and go chasing a man.

"Such a change in you, Miss Pearsall." Mrs. Desmond had turned abruptly to Mara. "I cannot believe it! You are very pale. Did you lose weight due to illness?"

Mara only gazed at her with indifference. "No, ma'am," she said politely.

Gaylord was frowning at her, as though admonishing her to speak up more, but there was nothing she wished to say to the woman.

"But you are very pale, though you were always gray and pallid. The Spanish air, I expect, not like dear England!" She turned to Gaylord with a little sparkling laugh and gazed up with green eyes into his face. "Dear Gaylord, remember the fine mornings, with dew on the grass, when we went riding in the country? There was nothing like that, the old days!"

He smiled politely, and Mara, watching, thought she saw mockery as he gazed down lazily at the woman beside him. "Oh, the mornings here are quite fine, Vivienne, if you rise early enough! There is dew on the thick grass and flowers aplenty. Only I am years older, and wearier! With wars behind me. One has to change with the times, and experiences. Don't you find it so, Vivienne?"

She flushed unbecomingly. Enid rushed in quickly with some conversation. "Oh, but I find the mornings quite as beautiful as ever! While we were still in the country house in England, we would ride out each morning, Lyman and I, when he was home. We would ride for miles, sometimes overlooking the farms, and combining business with pleasure—" And then a shadow crossed her pretty face.

Another English lady chimed in with reminiscences of England, and the conversation became general. But Mara noticed how Vivienne Desmond kept seeking Gaylord's attention, with a ringed hand on his sleeve, a bright glance up to his face, a girlish laugh, an intimate remark made low only to him. He seemed to enjoy the attentions, she thought, with contempt. She wondered idly if Mrs. Desmond loved Gaylord, or wanted his money—or if Gaylord was not wealthy, and he was interested in the rich widow—That was the way society was.

Thank God, her father had done that for her, thought Mara. He had left her a fortune, so she need not marry for money, or marry when she did not wish! No matter what Gaylord did to her, he could not force her to a priest, as José had said.

The ladies finally left, and Gaylord returned to the drawing room, stretching his long arms with a gesture of relief. "Paaa! Those long hours of talking of nothing! I detest small talk. Mara, come and look at horses with me! I like horses; they do not try to talk to me!"

Jennie giggled and begged to come along, but Enid was firm. Gaylord tucked Mara's shawl about her, the white one for the white dress, and pulled her with friendly rudeness with him. "Oh, come on, Mara, forget your temper, and leave it behind! Don't you like horses?"

"Well—yes, I do," she admitted, and came along. Her white slippers kept up with his quick-booted strides. Her white dress fluttered in the sunshine of the bright October day, as they walked around the graveled paths back to the stables and fenced-in pastures.

They went to lean on a fence and contemplate the beautiful blacks and grays. Gaylord studied them keenly, seeming to forget Mara. "There— look at that one, Mara. A fine mare, isn't she? From the south here. We had thoroughbreds with us, you know, helped us in spying on the enemy. Wellington depended on our reports, you can imagine. Those horses got us away from any patrol! No one could catch up with us!"

So that had been his work, she thought keenly, her mind suddenly turned from horses to the late wars. Gaylord had been one of Wellington's bright young officers, probably assigned to reconnaissance, spying on the French troops and their movements, bringing reports to the Commander in Chief. And she had run with the guerrillas, doing much of the same work. It was odd they had never encountered each other. But he would not have recognized her, if he had seen her a dozen times. She had always worn boys' clothing, and a cap to cover her hair, riding like a young man.

Gaylord whistled softly, coaxingly. The black mare perked up her ears, shivered, then trotted over to him, to stand nervously as he stroked her silky neck. "Touch her, Mara, she will stand still for you."

Mara reached up and stroked the fine animal, smiling at the wide frightened dark eyes as they calmed. "Oh, you are a love, you are a beauty," she said in Spanish.

"She is yours," said Gaylord.

Mara stared at him. "Mine?" But—she felt such a strange joy, such a feeling—no one had ever given her a present like this. "Mine?"

"Yes. There is but one condition," he added, with a twisted smile. "That riding habit, the blue velvet one with the plumed hat—"

She stiffened, outraged. "Oh, no, you would not—"

"Oh, yes, I would, Mara! I would bribe you! The mare is yours, and you may have her as your own—only whenever you ride her you must wear the blue riding habit and the plumed hat, or something equally grand and beautiful, to show off your lovely figure!"

She dropped her hand from the mare's neck and turned about, but the mare, overcoming her fright, ducked down and nuzzled at Mara as she would leave. Impulsively the girl turned again and flung her arms about the mare's neck and hugged her.

"There, it is a bargain!" said Gaylord, with immense satisfaction. "Run and change, and I'll take you for a ride at once!"

Mara made a face at him, her gamine grimace. Gaylord stared at her, then burst out laughing with good humor. "Run, or I'll spank you!" he threatened. She ran.

She changed to the blue velvet habit, put on the hat with plumes, cut off Juana's exclamations of how attractive she was, and ran down, to find Gaylord had had the mare saddled, also his own favorite gray stallion, and was waiting for her. She swung on and was off like a bird, calling a challenge to him to catch her, and he followed her.

When they finally slowed down from the fine gallop, he said, "You ride very well, much better than I had expected! Now, nod and smile to those gentlemen coming toward us!"

Mara scowled and pulled up, glancing uncertainly about her for another way to go. Gaylord caught at the reins below her hand and led her on. He forced her to be polite to them for a few minutes before they went on.

They rode often after that, usually in the early mornings, but always she was frozen toward the men they met. She would ignore their stares as much as she could, thinking Gaylord could force her and bribe her to dress up—but he could not force her to endure the courtship of any of these fops!

CHAPTER 5

"I think you like your new fine clothes, señorita," Juana exclaimed one evening, as Mara was dressing.

Mara swung on her. "Enjoy them. Enjoy them! You are mad! I hate them, and I hate him for making me wear them—"

Juana was beaming with maddening complacency. "You would not have to wear them. You could hide behind illness, or some such device as you used with your father. No, you are a woman, an attractive lady, and you enjoy it. You may scowl at the men, and frown at compliments, but secretly you look at the mirror, and you think 'Can this be me?' And you like the way you look!"

"Oh, Juana," Mara groaned. She was too honest to deny it. She stole another look at the new self in the mirror, at the vivid blue satin dress, the stunning sapphire bracelet on her wrist—another of Gaylord's presents—and sighed. She saw behind her the reflection of her middle-aged duenna,

Juana, smiling at her, and impulsively turned and hugged her, her cheeks burning. "Is it so obvious that I am different?" she asked wistfully.

"Different? You are a butterfly changed from a worm. You are a bird taking wing and flying in the blue sky. You are your true self, the self you were meant to be, the self God meant you to become. You could not hide it forever. God bless you."

Overcome with emotion, Juana kissed her cheek as lovingly as a mother, and Mara clung to her, this kindly woman who had cared for her and worried over her and clucked at her since she had come to Madrid, a lost, bewildered, hurt child of twelve.

"There now, you must not keep *him* waiting. He will be furious with you—until he sees how pretty you look tonight!"

No need to ask who *he* was. Juana was much in awe of Gaylord Humphrey, lost in admiration of his ways with her difficult charge. He had succeeded in a few days where others had failed for years, to change her scrawny, defiant, pecking duckling into a swan. And such a swan. Juana smoothed the blue-black hair lovingly, shaped the long curl that fell over the creamy shoulder, as Mara added the long dangling sapphire earrings, that matched her bracelet.

There was a hard knock at the door of the outer room. "I am coming, I am coming!" Juana called, and rushed to the other door. "Yes, sir, she is ready! Come in, sir!"

Mara scowled at her own lovely reflection in the mirror and picked up the silvery fan she had decided to carry on her wrist. Deliberately she waited another few minutes, then picked up her blue velvet cloak and walked out of the bedroom. The vivid blue eyes went to her at once; she endured his long critical stare as he studied her.

"Well, will I do, sir, will I do to entice the next longing suitor who would dearly love to marry the heiress?" she defied him, hurling the words at him like bullets.

Unexpectedly he smiled gently at her, whimsically. His moods were more varied and more unpredictable than her own, she thought. "You will do, Mara. You look lovely. Now, if I could only persuade you to smile enticingly—"

Deliberately she tilted her chin, fluttered her long dark lashes as she had seen Mrs. Desmond do, and smiled, slowly, entrancingly, as she had practiced in front of a mirror. "Like—that—sir?" she murmured, her voice sultry.

He stared, then burst out laughing. "Just like that, Mara! Lord, Lord, the child has grown up, eh, Juana? Come along, and we shall see them fall over to their faces before you!"

It was not the admiration and awe she had expected. She stiffened in outrage, glared at him, her blue eyes flashing. Still laughing, he took her arm and led her out the door.

She had not expected the evening to be a pleasant one, rather a frightening one. Gaylord had accepted an invitation to the house of Lope Sanchez-Garcia. She had protested, but could not give her real reason for refusing. He had flatly refused to accept any of her weak excuses.

Yet a challenge always excited her, so she went out with her chin up, one of her prettiest dresses on, and a smile on her lips. Enid exclaimed over her, looking beautiful herself in a pale blue silk which set off her blonde beauty.

Lyman Chandler was silent in their carriage as they set out. He was a big ponderous man, always absorbed in business interests, and as Mara had come to know fluttery excitable Enid, she did not wonder that the woman's attention had strayed. She longed for romance, thrills, intrigue over a fan, pretty music, dancing. Lyman Chandler went reluctantly to balls, was rarely at teas, was silent at dinner parties. Their marriage had been arranged by their parents, Mara had discovered, and she felt more than ever like fighting against Gaylord's arrangements for his ward.

"The Sanchez-Garcia home is one of the old ones of Madrid," Enid was telling Mara. "They say it is full of ghosts! I know the armor in the hallway is formidable! I always think there might be ghosts in them—or blood on the swords, or something."

"Nonsense, Enid," said Lyman, rousing from his abstraction. "No such thing. More likely the dungeons have torture instruments in them, from the Inquisition, nothing more than that."

Both the ladies shuddered. Mara thought of the thin cruel lips of Sanchez-Garcia, the light tormenting of Cristobal and his glittering eyes as she had given the order—no, she would not think of that tonight. The wars were over.

"But perhaps Mara is more familiar than we are with the Sanchez-Garcia home," suggested Gaylord gently, from his seat opposite Mara in the carriage. "Do you know it, Mara?"

"I have been there, in the old days. We played sometimes in the summerhouse, outside the ballroom," she admitted.

There was silence until they reached the home in the residential area of Madrid. The house itself was behind a high stone wall, and the gardens were dark, the house as full of shadows as Mara's own home had been, before she came to La Casa Dorada. She and Enid left their cloaks with one of the attentive maids and proceeded to the ballroom, where their escorts waited for them. Mrs. Desmond was already fluttering about Gaylord, Mara was quick to note.

She was smiling and chatting, but her smile was frozen as Gaylord turned to Mara and asked, "The first dance, child? As my ward?" And he swept her into his arms before she could object. Around his shoulder, for he was too tall for her to see over it, she could see Mrs. Desmond's furious eyes before she turned away.

Mara had heard more gossip, mostly from Jennie. It seemed that Vivienne St. Claire had married a wealthy man named Paul Desmond, and Jennie thought that her Uncle Gaylord had been mad and gone off to wars because of it. "Then his uncle, my great-uncle, died, and left Uncle Gaylord his money and the title, and was *she* furious. Now she comes around like honey to the beehive, only Uncle Gaylord is making her wait for the honey," said Jennie brightly, with satisfaction, rolling the words around her small pink lips.

How much honey? Mara wondered as Gaylord swirled her about the candle-lit ballroom. She swayed and dipped in his arms, her natural grace taking to the animated waltz. She felt the iron hardness of his arm as he supported her in the turns, felt the warmth of his chest as he pulled her close for a moment, saw the flush in his tanned cheeks as he held her away and gazed down at her. She wondered if she were as flushed from the dancing as he was.

How much honey? Did Gaylord spend so extravagantly because he had the money, or wanted more? She was wise enough to know the ways of society. She had overheard much from the pantry of her father's home, as the guests gossiped over the latest bit of relishing news. Mrs. Desmond was not very wealthy; she had run through much of her husband's money already. Did she want Gaylord—or his money—or were both deceiving each other? That would be ironically funny, if they should marry each other for money, only to find each had been fooled! She half-smiled, and Gaylord smiled down at her.

"There—now your face is pretty," he said with satisfaction.

She flushed and was glad when the dance was ended, and he released her to a Spaniard, an older man who had known her father. She was whirled then from one man to another, the Spaniards, the British, the Viennese, the Prussians, even some French who had fought on the "wrong side," and now stayed to enjoy their triumph.

It was about eleven o'clock, when Mara finally retreated to one of the rooms set aside for the ladies, to repair her make-up, look at her hair, adjust her dress, fan her flushed cheeks. She saw no one she knew. She had not seen Enid for over an hour, she realized.

A black-clad neat maid sidled up to her, slid a paper into her hands, as she sat before a mirror. "Señorita—for you. A small note, in secret," she said, and smiled with the happy intrigue of maids.

Mara nodded. She was stiff. She retreated to a dark corner and unrolled the paper. "In the summerhouse—urgent. José." She read it and read it again, then stuffed the note into her low-cut bodice. She picked up her fan and went out.

What could have gone wrong? She had talked to José today about the evening; he had been somewhat concerned. Perhaps he had heard something; he had some warning for her.

She knew the house; she had a memory for such details as the location of the back stairs, the placing of doors, the rooms and their arrangements. She went down the back stairs, encountering only a busy footman, and went quietly to one of the back drawing rooms from which she could leave to go to the summerhouse. She slipped out and closed the French doors after her. The night air was chill. She hesitated, almost went back for her cloak, then braved it to go on. He had said "urgent."

There was a lightened stone path to the summerhouse, leading from the open French windows of the ballroom. She hesitated again, then turned and made her way around to the back of the house, and around another way. It was an instinct from the war years that she had always obeyed.

She stole up to the back of the large summerhouse and peered into the shadows. Someone was there—but who? She thought she saw a light dress. A woman?

A hand closed over her wrist. She started, turned. "José!" she whispered.

"Hush. Yes, what is it? Why did you write me a note to meet you here?"

She stared up at his anxious face and went chill. "I did not—José, I have a note from you. A trap—yes?"

"Yes. Let us retreat quickly."

They both heard the voices at the same time. The murmured broken exclamation of the woman, a man's deeper tones. Enid—and Ramón Olivera!

"Kiss me again," he ordered in Spanish. "Tell me—tell me what I have longed to hear—

"Ramón—Ramón—I love you—I adore you—"

Mara's mouth tightened in disgust and pity. She tugged at José's arm, for them to leave. Then she saw the figures approaching from the other side of the summerhouse. Three men—and they were going to enter the house!

In the lights streaming from the huge home, she saw clearly the cruel triumphant face of Lope Sanchez-Garcia—and the lean blond handsomeness of Gaylord Humphrey! The other man—he was one of the British staff.

The trap was about to spring—but the wrong couple was inside. Swiftly Mara tugged José forward, and she caught at Enid's arm. As the woman swung around, she put a hand over her mouth.

"Quickly—Mrs. Chandler—return to the ballroom. José will conduct you! Quickly—leave—that way!" Her hands were like steel as she tugged the woman away. "José—to the ballroom, then leave! I can take care of myself! Go—go!"

The two left swiftly by the back way. Mara swung on the pale trembling handsome guardsman.

"Take me in your arms—at once!" she ordered, and moved closer to him. His arms closed about her automatically, and she raised her face to his provocatively—as a light shone on them.

"Here they are—your little ward! How charming—and her escort—Ah!" And by the tone of Sanchez-Garcia's voice, Mara could judge his disappointment. "What have we here?"

She turned about and saw the fury and disgust and amazement in Gaylord's face as he took in the scene—saw also the swift recovery, the suave mask descending as he recovered.

"Ah, we seem to have interrupted something—" the other Britisher was saying. "A little rendezvous—harmless—no spies here, señor!" He chuckled without humor, looking anxiously at Gaylord.

Gaylord seemed to have something else on his mind. "I say, Olivera, when I asked you to teach my fiancée some dancing, this was not what I had in mind!" he said, sounding disgusted. "I meant for you to take her to one of the drawing rooms and instruct her there! Mara, you will catch a chill out here!" He smoothly detached her from the shaking arm of the tall guardsman and put his arm about her.

"You did not say where we were to dance, Gaylord!" said Mara pertly, her own voice sounding strange in her ears. "And I don't relish observers when I am trying to learn all the latest dances. It is your own fault—I am not so interested in learning—"

"Quiet, ward," he said mockingly. "Since we are going to be married, it is time you learned not to question my decisions!"

"Married?" asked Sanchez-Garcia. "This is the first I had heard of it!"

"Of course. We fell in love at once, but of course, it is not yet announced," said Gaylord smoothly. "I had told Olivera to teach her some dances, but this was not what I had in mind! Ah, well, I had best teach her myself! Come on, Mara, back to the ballroom! And why did you not wear your cloak, love? You are quite cold!"

"Well—I say—this is a surprise. Catch of the season, lovely heiress—and Gaylord has snatched her up!" The other Britisher, obviously relieved, was chatting on, chuckling to his ominously silent host.

Mara was walking beside Gaylord. He might sound smooth and happy, but she knew by the tightness of his arm about her, the tension of his hand on her wrist, the tautness of his whole body, that he was furious with her.

He had saved her reputation by his quick thinking, but she was going to have to pay! And she could not save herself by telling about the notes—or about his own sister's rendezvous with the guardsman.

Mara had learned loyalty in a hard school, and the lessons were imprinted deeply on her. She would not betray Enid. But she wondered what she would have to pay to Gaylord.

CHAPTER 6

Gaylord was most attentive to Mara the rest of the evening. Somehow the news of their engagement had swept through the ballroom, and to Mara's disgust, Gaylord did not deny it. He accepted congratulations with smiling politeness and squeezed her waist if she was slow in responding to remarks. She was furious with him by the time they left the dance.

She went right to bed, but not to sleep. She was fairly certain who had sent the notes. Sanchez-Garcia was trying to discredit her with Gaylord and trap her and José together. They must be on guard. As for the fake engagement—she would soon end that!

She tossed and turned in her soft bed, thinking over the evening. She always returned to the same thought—how angry Gaylord must be! And what control he had over his face and emotions, that he had so quickly recovered and smoothed over the incident, making up the story of the engagement and her dancing.

He was more clever than she had estimated—José had been right about him. She would have to be on her guard.

She finally slept, but poorly, until morning, when she slept deeply and did not waken until late. The sunshine was streaming through her pale blue curtains when she finally yawned and opened her eyes. She blinked at the light and pulled the bell rope.

Juana came in, beaming, to open the curtains for her. "Ah, what excitement, señorita! My little one engaged!"

"Not at all, all foolishness," Mara muttered crossly, and sat up, stretching. "Ah—it is late, I think. I will have my breakfast in my rooms. I don't want to see anyone!"

"You will eat, and then the lord wishes to see you in his study, señorita," said Juana cheerfully, and went to draw her bath.

Mara scowled. So he was issuing more orders to her! She went to take her bath, soaked deliberately a long time in the warmth, then dressed in the muslin gown of pale blue that Juana had set out. She fastened it at her waist with the ribbons of deep blue, then Juana brushed her hair and tied it with a matching deep blue ribbon.

They both started when a deep voice called from the next room, "Mara, are you dressed yet? May I come in?"

"No, you may not!" she called furiously, and jumped up and ran to the door, and pushed it open. She would not put it past his impudence to come into her bedroom! She glared at Gaylord, standing smiling in the midst of her sitting room.

"I have not yet had breakfast," she said crossly.

"Is that why your temper is so bad? Juana, fetch her coffee and some sweet cakes, to sugar her! Run, she is in an immensely ferocious temper!" And he dared to laugh down at Mara's scowling face.

Juana giggled and left the room.

Mara tried to get control of herself. She walked over to her favorite lounge chair and sat down, studying his face cautiously. He seemed quite cheerful this morning, not cross or belligerent. What was he up to?

"You have not greeted your fiancé properly, Mara, darling, but we will let that go for the present. I came up to bring you an engagement ring." And he walked over to her and took her hand.

"What—what—you are mad!" She tried to snatch her hand from his, but he gripped her small fingers tightly. He had taken a ring from his pocket, and even as she struggled, he slid the blazing sapphire on her hand. "You are absolutely mad! I am not going to be engaged to you! How dare you—take this off!"

He sat down beside her, so close that she

jumped nervously. "Calm yourself, child," he said quietly. "Do you realize that all Madrid is gossiping about us this morning? Of course you are engaged to me, did I not announce it? Don't you care about your reputation?"

"Not a fig," she said, but she went rather white. It was one thing to refuse to marry. It was quite another to have a ruined reputation in rigidly proper Spain. The society in England was lax enough, but usually it was the married women who carried on their loose affairs. A single girl was ruined forever if she did so.

"Of course you do," he said, in that same quiet tone. "You have acted foolishly, but I am not going to scold you. You are not accustomed to the ways of society, and that guardsman is quite a handsome fellow. However—he has been reprimanded and understands that his position is in danger if any more such incidents occur."

She flushed deeply and lowered her gaze to the flashing huge ring. It was heavy on her small hand, the huge sapphire set in some smaller diamonds in a circle. It was a beauty, and she might have admired it if—if it had been a true gift, and not the sign of a mock engagement.

"How—how long do we have to remain engaged, señor?" she finally asked stiffly. She could not betray Enid and her Ramón; he would lose his position, and Enid her precarious reputation.

"Are you so anxious to marry, my love?" he

said, a little mockingly. "Oh, I think we shall marry quite soon. I am not anxious for a long engagement either!"

"I did not mean that, and you know it! How long must we keep up the farce, señor?" She glared at him with flashing blue eyes. And he tapped her cheek maddeningly.

"It is not going to be a farce, my darling. And I think you had better practice saying my name! You will appear strange if you keep calling me señor! As to our marriage—I think we can plan matters for a month or two? What do you think?"

"You are jesting with me. I am serious!"

"So am I, Mara." He dropped her hand and stood up abruptly, looming over her. "I have decided. It is the best solution. It came to me last night. No other man in the world can handle you—you are a complicated and tricky and difficult woman! I cannot inflict you upon any unsuspecting young Englishman, and I cannot have you marry a Spaniard. I do not hate the Spaniards! So—I must keep the burden myself! As I said—we shall marry, and soon. You may as well get accustomed to the idea, Mara!" And he made her a little mocking bow, his eyes blazing down at hers.

"You—are—mad!" she whispered, catching her breath. "You cannot be serious! I will never marry you."

"Never is a long time, Mara. Get used to the

idea. Oh—after your breakfast, come down to the study. I have some papers of your father's, and we might as well wind up matters soon. When we marry, we will have other things to occupy our time!" And he walked out of the room abruptly as Juana came in with her breakfast tray.

Juana set down the breakfast tray and then saw her face. "My little Mara, what is the trouble, my dove? What is it, my sparrow?" She touched Mara's face coaxingly, her dark face anxious.

"He—he—he says he—is going to marry me!" Mara whispered, her hands clasped tightly together. The huge ring bit into her fingers.

"But of course! Are you not engaged? And the ring, oh, lovely dove, what a beautiful ring. He gives you fine, beautiful presents, no? He adores you, no? He cannot remain away from you, is it not true?" To Juana, it was all clear and quite inevitable. The fine lord had looked at Mara and fallen in love with her, and of course he wanted to marry her.

Mara sighed, picked at her breakfast and wanted to flee to José. But he was giving lessons, and Gaylord sent another impatient message for her to come to his study—the lawyers were waiting!

So she went slowly downstairs, to find that Gaylord was indeed serious. He had an English lawyer and a Spanish one, and they had papers and law books spread before them, ready to settle matters from her father's estate. She was irritated at first, then she began to realize that her problems with her father's papers had arisen because the matters were indeed complicated.

"If you will wait a few minutes, gentlemen," she said, finally, in relief, "I will go upstairs to my rooms and bring the remainder of his papers. There are some which might throw light on this."

She sped upstairs, then returned with the papers. When Gaylord saw them and how she had worked on them, he said reproachfully, "But Mara, why did you not tell me what you were doing? I could have told you what a task it would involve!"

She set her small chin, her mouth tightening. "I could do it myself," she said stubbornly.

The men exchanged telling glances, and her self-styled "fiancé" shook his blond head. "What a one," he muttered. "No, Mara, leave it to us. We will straighten it all out."

The other men agreed. She was irritated, yet relieved, to have the immense pile of legal and financial matters out of her hands. After two hours, the men agreed to have the lawyers take the papers with them and try to get order out of their chaos.

"And you, Mara, after lunch you must have a long siesta. You are looking weary," said Gaylord, with what she thought was assumed tenderness. "Get some sleep. I want you bright for the ball tonight."

"Another ball? My God, Gaylord," she said bluntly. "We cannot go out every night. I shall be exhausted!"

He put his hand on the back of her neck, shook her lightly, and laughed down at her. The lawyers were smiling indulgently.

"My wife could dance every night of the week," muttered the Spaniard, with a sigh.

"Mara will learn," said Gaylord, with infuriating calm. She tried to duck away from his hand. His fingers only clasped her more tightly.

He finally let her go, but it was at his own choosing, she thought later, at luncheon. Enid was unusually quiet, Gaylord seemed to be deep in thought, and for once they did not have guests.

Gaylord finally said, "I am not sure what I will have you wear tonight, Mara. I will come up later and choose for you. Our engagement will be announced formally tonight. I have arranged it with our hosts."

She tossed back her head, her wide eyes meeting his. "But—I told you—we said—I mean, I am not—"

He interrupted her deliberately. "I know, Mara. But I think I am a better judge of which dresses are most attractive on you. I will come up after your siesta."

He rose from the table, excused himself, and

departed. He left Mara biting her lips, Enid looking at Mara curiously. Mara did go to José then, to find him thoughtful. He had heard the news.

"Well, I suppose it will do no harm to remain engaged for a time. That Mrs. Desmond is a vicious gossip. If she thought you were having an affair with Ramón, she would rip you to pieces! She still thinks to catch Gaylord."

"She can have him! They deserve each other!" she said spitefully.

"And you, little Mara. Do you not find him most attractive? He is a handsome lord. He has never married, his war record is heroic, he fights well, he commands well. He has many qualities you have admired."

Mara stared at José. "You cannot be serious! You know I hate men! I never wish to marry. And that man—he is dominating, hateful, he drives me mad! He wishes to order me about, he forces me to wear these—these clothes!" She pulled out the skirt of her muslin dress. The sapphire ring flashed on her hand.

José smiled faintly. "And you, Mara, you accept this? You do not rip off the dresses, feign illness, faint, pout, bite, and scratch!"

"With that one it would do no good," she said frankly. "I think he would only spank me!"

José burst out laughing. "Maybe he is the one for you then! No, no, little one, I am only teasing! Patience, wait for him to show his hand. Perhaps he does not really want to marry you. Perhaps he only draws on that Mrs. Desmond and shows her he is not ripe for her plucking. Wait and see what his game is."

With that advice she withdrew to her room, to find that Juana had darkened it, with orders from Gaylord that her charge was to rest. Mara undressed, put on her white negligee and flung herself down sulkily to do just that.

She went to the ball that night in the dress which Gaylord had chosen for her. It was of blue satin, with flounces of black Spanish lace, in a stunning combination of English design and Spanish inspiration. Gaylord had directed that her hair be set high, with curls falling from her crown, and in the curls was set a black delicate lace mantilla fastened with a flashing comb of brilliants. She wore his sapphires, including the engagement ring.

She was complimented by Spaniards and English alike. Gaylord endured all this for a time, then swept her away with him in a dance, whirling her round and round the room.

"I am glad I have to get engaged only once," he told her, with a devilish look in his deep blue eyes. "We shall get married swiftly and be done with all this ceremony! Right, Mara? Don't you dislike all the ceremony?"

She was outraged. He had worded it so cleverly that she could not agree or disagree with him.

Her blue eyes flashed up to meet his. He laughed aloud, ducked down, and kissed her boldly on her creamy throat, under her ear.

"There, I have been wanting to kiss that place. It is delicious," he said, and pressed his warm lips to it again.

"Don't do that!" she scolded weakly, feeling warm and strange.

"But we are engaged, Mara, darling," and he laughed again and whirled her about until she was dizzy.

He monopolized her dancing time outrageously, whirling her away from would-be suitors who protested in French, Spanish, English, Russian, that he could not take away the pretty lady.

"The pretty lady belongs to me," he laughed back at them.

"Really, Gaylord, you are being rude now," she protested, her cheeks flushed a bright pink, and her eyes amazingly starry. She felt so odd, to be held so closely, to be frankly hugged in the dance, to be brazenly claimed by him again and again. Her mind was in a turmoil. She did not know if she hated him or—

He whirled her to a quiet drawing room and danced about the room with her until she was dizzy again. "Oh—stop—stop—I cannot see—" she finally gasped, and clasped his arms to make him pause.

"Can you not, love?" He drew her close, and

when she closed her eyes against the whirling room, he bent down. His mouth closed passionately over hers, and she was held breathless for a long, long moment in time. His mouth was insistent, warm, opened, pressed hotly to hers, and her body was drawn tightly to his. She felt his heat, his quickened breathing, as though they were her own.

She finally began to struggle, frightened of her own emotions; she had never known such strange feelings in her life. She wanted to melt against him, she wanted—wanted—She struggled more violently, rejecting herself as well as him.

She finally managed to pull away from him, and he held her at arms' length, studying her face. His face was flushed, his mouth hard and sweet. Her eyes were wide, frightened, gazing up at his.

"No—no—no," she was saying. "I hate you. I hate you! You must not—I cannot endure it—" She was close to crying, and tears came to her eyes. She tried to strike at him, he caught at her wrists and held them tightly.

"Mara, you must calm down. Mara! Listen to me. You do not hate me. I will not have it so!"

She did not listen to him, trying distractedly to pull away with her strength, which was usually so sturdy, but seemed frail and useless against his steel. "I hate you, I hate you—I hate your kisses! You have no right—"

"I have the right. I claim the right. You belong to me."

"No—no—I hate men. I despised my father. The way he treated my mother—he left her—he left her, and she was so gentle, so hurt, she could not even fight—" And now she was really crying, hating her tears, but unable to prevent them.

"Mara, listen to me. Your mother asked for it, she was too dull and meek. She should have fought for him! But she would not. But you—Mara—you are like your father. You have his eyes, his spirit! You are like your father! I can see him in you, and you make me—" He paused abruptly, staring down at her. "Ah—but not now," he seemed to caution himself. "Not now. Mara, listen to me, love. You must be more calm. Accept this—"

And he tried to draw her close to him again. This time she fought him, with tight mouth, hard fists, kicking out at him with her thin slippers, until he finally gave up. "I will not, I will not, I hate you, I hate you—" she kept saying over and over.

Finally he shook her, and her hair began to come loose from its curls and stream down over her shoulders. He seemed to collect himself, and her.

"Very well, Mara. Be calm. Look, here is a mirror. Your hair, I will arrange it again, so." And he drew her over to a mirror, and as patiently as Juana, he set her curls up again, fastened in the comb more closely, arranged the mantilla about her creamy bare shoulders with a lightly caressing touch. Behind her sulky tear-streaked face, she could see his tall figure, his tanned face, his intent eyes as he worked, and she felt a strange thrill, of anger, or fury?

She did not know what she felt, only that she was upset and confused, and shaking.

CHAPTER 7

When Mara finally fell asleep that night, she dreamed that she was in a dark night, black Spanish darkness all about her. She was riding, riding on the black mare that Gaylord had given her. But she was not in her riding habit, or the boyish clothing she had worn. She was wearing a white Spanish dress of lace—it was a wedding dress with a white veil.

In her dream she was frantic, riding, riding, trying to escape, she did not know what. But she rode right into a trap; masked horsemen stopped her, surrounded her. She cried out and turned— to find Gaylord behind her, standing with that strange look on his face that she had seen at the ball.

Something tender, something hard, something cruel and kind, something determined and passionate and—what? He held out his arms to her and said, "Mara, love, do not fret! Calm yourself, calm—" And she wakened as he was helping her down, and she was sliding down into his arms.

She sat up with a jerk, staring into the night darkness of her bedroom. What had it meant? At the last, from fright and panic she had been approaching happiness, an odd ecstasy, a delight, to be sliding down into Gaylord's arms—

Finally she fell asleep again, but the dream did not recur. Instead she seemed to be walking endlessly in a garden of roses and pansies and pinks, an English garden, all light and sunshine, with trimmed green hedges—walking, walking—as she had as a child.

She wakened early and lay trying to think. Why did Gaylord insist he was going to marry her? He was not in love with her, she thought. Why, then? Her money?

This was an expensive house, and he owned two others in England, one in London and one in the country. Perhaps he was deeply in debt, though his uncle had left him a fortune and title. That might be it. He knew exactly the extent of Mara's fortune, and he might covet it. Mrs. Desmond had some money, but she was extravagant. He might want Mrs. Desmond, but was too cold-blooded to marry without big prospects of fortune.

She sat up in bed, thinking, her hands clasped about her knees, her loose hair tossed and disheveled. She brushed it back from her shoulders impatiently—and abruptly remembered the touch of Gaylord's hands as he had carefully arranged her curls after kissing her and shaking her. She felt a hot blush burning through her. "Oh—oh—he is a devil!" she muttered uneasily.

She rang for Juana, got up and bathed. She was the first one down for breakfast and crept softly past the open door of Gaylord's study on the way to the breakfast room. Her caution was in vain. He looked up, stood, and came to follow her to the breakfast room.

He caught up with her just inside the door. "You are abroad early, my love," he said, with his teasing smile. No one was in the room. She turned to face him, feeling somehow at bay.

He came up to her, cupped her face in his hands and looked down into her eyes. Then slowly he bent and pressed his mouth to hers. She stiffened, was about to fight him, when he released her and went over to the bell rope and rang for the footman.

"What will you have this morning, Mara?" he asked, as casually as though he had not just pressed a burning kiss onto her lips. Her mouth still stung from it.

"C-coffee, p-please," she said, and went to her place. Just as he was releasing her, he had pressed her dark hair back from her face with an unmistakably caressing touch. Why, why, why did he keep on touching her like that, when he knew she hated it?

"I should like to take you to the dressmaker's

again today, Mara," he said from his seat.

"Again? I have not worn half the clothes you ordered, Gaylord! Really, what is the need—" she asked impatiently.

"I enjoy it. It is like dressing a pretty doll," he said with a smile.

"But I hate trying on things, and I don't want any more clothes, and—and besides, I am busy—"

"I have ordered some purple velvet from Señora Rodriguez. We shall try that color on you. I think we shall find," he added blandly, helping himself to the steaming meat dish the footman held for him, "that your eyes are not as blue as sapphires, but rather as purple as pansies. Thank you," he added to the footman.

She could feel the color stealing into her cheeks. She kept her gaze on her food, but did not see it. She tried to drink her coffee; it burned her mouth, and she set the cup down hastily.

Lyman Chandler came in, and the conversation became less personal, to her great relief. Enid came in later, yawning, and the conversation turned to some visits she might make to a new English family just arriving in Madrid.

She escaped when she could, only to be recalled to the drawing room within an hour for some early morning visitors. She was surprised to find that one of the ladies was Mrs. Vivienne Desmond.

"Really, Vivienne," drawled Enid, in one of her

rare catty remarks. "One would think you are quite drawn to us. I have never known you to rise so early, so often! Have you quite reformed?"

The woman flushed an ugly red, and her green eyes snapped. Her smile would have curdled fresh milk, thought Mara, quite fascinated.

"Actually, I came early because I have so much to do today. A visit to my dressmaker, then a call on a Russian princess this afternoon. But first, I thought I must speak to Mara." Mrs. Desmond tried to smile more naturally and went over to sit beside the girl.

Mara tried not to stiffen. She disliked the woman, distrusted her. But her curiosity led her on, as it had during the wars, when she felt danger tingling down her spine and clues bristling in conversation, when she had listened at doors and opened letters, and ridden like the wind through the countryside at night to carry news that might be important.

"I cannot imagine what you must speak to me about," she said softly, fluttering her lashes. If Mrs. Desmond thought her a green girl, so much the better.

Mrs. Desmond turned, so that the others might not overhear a chance remark. "You are so young, and you have been so sheltered. I thought it was my duty—I am older than you, I have known Gaylord for a long time, my dear!" She patted Mara's hand. Mara let her hand lie limp, though she knew the emerald gaze had fastened on the blue sapphire on that hand.

"I am sure you mean to be kind, Mrs. Desmond." Mara said that demurely, and thought how adept she was becoming at the social lie.

"Of course! Why else would I have rushed over here? I was so sure you would not listen to Gaylord, to his blandishments. Oh, he is so adept at turning a girl's head. He quite sweeps one off one's feet! How well I know him," and she sighed and smiled all at once, her gaze softening as though at some fond memories. "But oh, my dear—" and she returned to Mara seriously. "He is not to be trusted. He cannot be trusted. His attentions are as fickle as the wind. He blows hot, blows cold. I know it so well. Once—you may as well know it—once we were to have been married."

"Oh, really?" Mara opened her blue eyes widely, innocently. "And what happened, Mrs. Desmond? Did you meet someone else?"

The smile tightened, became fixed, then with an effort the older woman relaxed it. "Fortunately, yes. For Gaylord was about to drop me, as he did all women! He is a confirmed bachelor. And if he ever did marry, I have always thought he would be as unfaithful to his wife as he was to his—women friends. He is incapable of fixing his attention for long on one woman!"

"Indeed, this is very shocking," said Mara, and

tried hard to sound shocked. Inwardly, she was bubbling with laughter. The woman was so obvious! Did she think Mara had fallen for Gaylord's charms and kisses?

Then abruptly she remembered Gaylord's kisses of last night and this morning, and her very flesh seemed to burn where he had pressed his lips. She felt a heat sweeping over her, and she knew the hot color was coming into her cheeks. She pressed her hands together, striving for calm.

The woman's keen gaze did not miss her agitation, and she smiled. "Poor dear, I am shocking you," she murmured. "Listen, dear. Take my advice. Break the engagement gracefully—before he breaks it cruelly for you! He is never serious. I can tell you this. We understand each other, and he knows I always forgive him. He will return to me—he always does."

"Indeed?" asked Mara faintly, and now she felt cold. Her very hands were chilled. "He—always returns—"

"To me, yes. He returns after he wearies of the girls he chases, after the older women he takes as his mistresses—I am sorry to shock you, but it is true! He uses a woman, discards her. Oh, I am not saying he would use you, do not believe that! You are only a child, and his ward. But he is temporarily entranced with you. But—eventually he will come back to me once more. And I? Silly woman. I adore him, I always have, no matter what his faults. When he comes back, I always welcome him."

Jennie had wandered closer and closer, fascinated as always by the adult conversation. Now Mara started as the child put her hand on Mara's, covering the bright ring.

"Auntie Mara, would you like some tea now?" murmured the child, her bright gaze going first to Mara then to the green-eyed woman. "Mrs. Desmond, may I fetch more tea for you?"

"You are a kind child," smiled Mrs. Desmond. She rose gracefully, languidly, shaking out her green and white striped skirts. "No, I must be on my way. Goodbye, dear child," she added kindly to Mara. "Do write me a note if there is anything you wish to discuss: I shall be happy to give my advice any time—any time at all, dear!"

Mara watched the lady making her way out of the drawing room, pausing at Enid's side for some remark, shaking hands, kissing a cheek here, sketching a laugh there.

Jennie whispered, "I don't like her either, Auntie Mara. Why are your hands so cold? Was she mean?"

Mara looked at the bright-eyed curious child and tried to smile. "No, probably not," she said. "I think—I do not like society very much, Jennie! It makes me—very cold."

"Come near the fire, then," said the little girl.

"No—no, I think I shall—go to my rooms."

Mara rose and took her departure somewhat abruptly, and Jennie gazed after her with her wise eyes.

Mara paused at her own rooms only long enough to find a large white shawl to put about her. She was truly cold, shivering convulsively from time to time. She could not doubt Mrs. Desmond; the woman had known Gaylord for years, as she had said. So Gaylord was truly like her own father, flitting from mistress to mistress, picking up a girl only to drop her when he was bored. Gaylord himself had said he enjoyed dressing her; it was like dressing a doll.

"But I am not a doll," she said fiercely to herself. "I am a woman—a woman of feelings! I will not let him hurt me!"

She went up the back stairs to the next floor, then to the fourth and made her way to the schoolrooms. There she found José seated before the fire, comfortably correcting some papers of the children. He looked up with a smile, drew forward a chair for her.

"I have fallen into a soft life, Mara," he said gently, seeing her troubled look. "And you, my child? How goes your life?"

"Oh, badly, José, badly," she sighed. "I seem to be in such a fix. How did I get there? What have I done wrong?"

He pursed his lips and laid aside the papers. "A fix. So what has happened lately? Tell me."

She told him briefly about Mrs. Desmond and her advice, not revealing the extent of Gaylord's actions to Mara, how he had kissed her and held her. Somehow she could not tell even José about that. His gentle brown gaze studied her; his melancholy face did not change expression as she spoke.

When she had finished her account, she asked, "So how can I break the engagement quickly, José? How can I give back the ring, and—and all the clothes—and go back to the house? I cannot remain here! It is—is unbearable!"

"Ah, yes, I see," he said thoughtfully, and then gazed into the fire. After a long pause he said musingly, "Think, Mara. Do you trust this woman, Mrs. Desmond?"

"No," she answered promptly.

"Then how can you credit what she says? If you cannot trust the source, you must distrust the information from the source, you know that."

She smiled faintly. It was one of his first lessons in espionage for her. "Yes, I remember, José. You trained me well."

"So why do you promptly forget all my lessons, little one?"

She thought in turn, gazing at the fire. "But there must be smoke where there is fire. And he has the reputation—which my father had. And I know that was true! Father had many mistresses, he even—he even brought them—to the house," she added in a low tone, hating the memory of those brightly clad rouged females he had brought.

"Your father was a man of passions, not a cautious man. He did many things which a colder man would not have done," said José. "But do not judge all men by one man. There are many kinds of men."

She made a despairing gesture. "But what am I to think—about *him?* If he is not like my father, then what is he? He acts so—he—he is loose, a rake, a libertine—" She tried to whip up her passions against him, but she kept remembering his kisses on her throat, on her mouth, the feel of his steel arms holding her tightly to his heated body, the intensity of his caresses.

"I think, Mara," said José deliberately, "that he loves you. Yes, I think that he loves you. In that case he will have a care and a tenderness for you, and you will be protected always."

She stared at him, brushed back her hair, the warmth coming up in her face. "You think he—loves me? Why? Why?"

He smiled. "You are a lovely girl, in her first bloom. You are different, fresh, impulsive, generous. Perhaps you are the girl he has sought all his life. Who knows? At any rate, he gives you presents, sees that you are the most lovely person at every ball, studies the right colors for your clothes, arranges your hair, gives you jewels which complement your coloring—What else can one think?"

"I—I don't know what to think, José. Oh, advise me! I want to leave! Oh, if we could only return home together and let it be like the old days!" she cried out passionately. "If we could only ride together, you and I, in the night, under the stars, riding free and clear, with no one to stop us—"

"The old days are over, little one. And your devoted José must rest by the fireside and think of the old days as one recalls a dream, dimly. Ah—but the memory of that—"

"Yes, the memory? Go on!"

Mara started violently. The voice was close behind her. She jumped up, turned about. Gaylord stood there, glaring at her incredulously. "You—how did you—" She glanced past him at the door. It stood open.

"You are very careless in your choice of rendezvous, Mara! I heard enough to make me quite curious. What are those memories you share with —the tutor?" He was controlling himself by an extreme effort, she knew by the tightness of his mouth, the white line about his lips, the clenching and unclenching of his fists.

José said mildly, "It is not what you think, señor. Little Mara was my student for many years. We studied and rode together—"

"Under the stars, at night, señor?" sneered Gaylord. "Do you take me for a fool?"

There was a long intense silence. Mara felt the frightened pulse in her throat. She could say nothing. They still had enemies, the secrets were not theirs!

Gaylord was still staring at them, and she could not read his face. She stood rigidly; José was leaning heavily against the back of the chair. His wound had been bothering him again; she could not let Gaylord strike him.

"Let us come away and leave José to his papers. I am sorry I disturbed you, José, with my chattering," she said, and attempted a smile. Timidly, she put her hand on Gaylord's wrist and felt the jump of his muscle as she touched him. "Let us— go, señor. We can—talk later."

"Very well." He permitted her to lead the way from the room. She closed the door after them and led the way down the back stairs, down to her rooms on the second floor. Once there, he closed the door after them, standing with his back to it. "Now, Mara, you will perhaps explain why you visit the tutor and chatter with him for hours?"

She faced him bravely, her head high, her chin up, her eyes wary. "He is a friend, señor, a friend of long standing. I have confided in him, and he has been gracious enough to advise me, as an old—

er one to a younger. That is all."

"All?" His fists clenched, relaxed again. "All. That is all. You hate all men—but you confide in one like the tutor, you sit beside him at the fire, and stretch out your feet to the blaze and touch his arm. This does not seem like hatred, señorita! Have you perhaps some other explanation for visits to him?"

"None, señor. You may believe me or not! Only —I beg you not to inflict your anger—on José. On me, yes, but not on him! He is not well." She was biting her lips, hating to plead with him. She would not for herself, but for José she would.

Theirs was a deep friendship strengthened by the dangers they had gone through together. She would not allow any action of hers to endanger him, as she had not during the wars.

Gaylord turned with an abruptly pantherish gesture and strode toward her windows; he flung aside the curtains and gazed out into the rainy morning. She wondered what he saw in the gray skies, the stormy tumult of the winds and blowing leaves.

Finally he turned back, and his face was more calm. "Very well, Mara," he said quietly, a dangerous cool in his tone. "I accept your explanation. I must trust you, as you must trust me. However—I have come to a decision. We shall be married at once. I think I can arrange the wed-

ding for this next week. I will take you to the
dressmaker's and have her begin on your wedding
gown."

He smiled grimly as her hands flew to her
throat. She felt an intense turmoil in her veins;
the pulse at her throat was so wild it was like a
bird wanting to leave her and fly away. "Next—
week—but no, but no—I cannot—oh, I do not
want—"

"You will be ready to drive with me in fifteen
minutes, eh? Very well. We shall discuss our plans
on the way. Juana!" he roared out so suddenly
that Mara jumped. The maid appeared from the
bedroom. "Mara's cloak, her scarf. We drive out!"

"Yes, señor," said the maid, and her wide eyes
were almost as startled as Mara's.

CHAPTER 8

Mara found out anew that when Gaylord said something, he meant it. Her next few days were crammed with activities connected with her wedding.

She went to the dressmaker's almost every day, until life became so furiously busy that the dressmaker had to come to the Casa Dorada with her garments and work in a sewing room all day. The wedding dress was completed, the veil, the white velvet cloak. Other garments grew under the skillful fingers of the assistants, the white muslins, the pale blue silks, the rose satins.

Between fittings Mara was kept busy answering invitations, receiving guests, opening wedding gifts of such splendor and magnificence she was quite bewildered. Gaylord insisted on her resting each afternoon, for they went out or received guests every evening until midnight.

He was having a huge suite of rooms redecorated for them, and she peeped at them timidly, unable to believe she would actually live there. A huge sitting room of large windows and magnificent furnishings was being redone with pale blue silk walls and matching couch and chair coverings. Her own bedroom was of deeper blue and cream, with a mammoth four-poster canopied in vivid blue silk.

Gaylord had a huge bedroom of his own, she was relieved to see. It was of blue and gold, the bed even larger than hers. Between their rooms was a small hallway, and the door to the bathroom which they would share. His bedroom had a separate entrance off the main hall, or he could reach it through her bedroom.

Her own feelings were in a turmoil. She had tried again and again to protest to him against haste, against the marriage itself. He had said coldly, "Why, Mara? Why will you not marry me? Are your feelings engaged by José, or some other man?"

"No, oh, no, no one, there is no one—" she had protested. "I just do not wish to marry—oh, let me return to my home—I want to go home!"

"Why do you wish to go home? Who will visit you there?" he asked cruelly, holding her wrist tightly in his hard fingers, his gaze searching her face. She did not know if he was truly jealous of her, or was angry at her defiance, or trying to do his duty as her guardian. She did not know what to think, and he did not tell her his true emotions.

"I want—to leave. I want to go alone—I want to live alone—" she had protested.

"You need someone to look after you," he said, and she thought he was coldly teasing. "You are incapable of looking after yourself! You would only get into trouble. You invite trouble, Mara, with your inviting eyes and your innocent mouth!" Then he laughed, dropped her wrist, and turned away abruptly.

Enid was sweetly helpful, taking a fascinated interest in the wedding preparations. She was practical also, suggesting tactful ways of handling the flood of wedding gifts. She set her own maid to unwrapping them, making sure the cards were displayed with them, preparing lists for Mara to study and answer later.

Mara was so confused she scarcely knew which way to turn. She dared not risk another visit to José. If Gaylord discovered her in the schoolroom with José one more time, she thought he would kill José. Or dismiss him with no character, and poor José would have no one to turn to. She could not risk that.

Small Jennie was delighted with the wedding in her own house. She ran about, as messenger for Mara, as chattering small attendant as guests came, whispering names importantly if Mara forgot one, clinging to her side, reveling in her own importance as a bridesmaid or flower girl. She was to be the only attendant; Mara refused to hear of any procession.

This was practically the only decision Mara made in that week. All other matters were settled by Gaylord, frequently before Mara had even heard of them. The church wedding, the reception, even her own wedding gown were decided by him.

The gown—she donned it with trembling hands on her wedding morning. She had breakfasted alone in her room, her last morning alone, she thought, and wondered at her shaking hands and chilled body. She had sat long in the blue negligee, thinking, thinking, until she thought she would run mad! Why was Gaylord marrying her? Because he wanted her money in addition to his own? To show Mrs. Desmond she could not control him? To dominate Mara, the one girl who dared defy him, who did not fall instant victim to his charm? Why, why, why?

She had tried to picture how life would be with him after the wedding, but it made her so afraid, so upset, she dared not risk thinking of it. Would he dominate her, treat her cruelly, then forget her to let her retire into the background of his life? Or—or what? What could he do to her? She would not act as her mother had done, weeping at his neglect! She would be glad of his neglect, as he turned to his mistresses, she thought, her mouth tight and hard and cynical.

Juana was hovering around, waiting to dress her. "Dove, my darling, you must not be late to your own wedding, my pearl," she urged, and Mara finally got up reluctantly.

The beautiful long satin undergarments, then the magnificent white dress which had hung in Mara's dress cupboard for two days. Of white Spanish lace, tier on tier, it clung to her arms and breasts, to her narrow waist, then fell in softest foaming waves of lace from her waist to her ankles, with the tiers of lace gently laid each on each. Her hair was dressed high in the curls Gaylord favored, and to the crown was attached the white sheer spiderweb lace veil. It fell about her shoulders and arms, almost to her waist, when Juana drew it forward.

Mara threw it back impatiently, to stare at her white face. "No, no, I am too white," she muttered, and lifted the little rouge brush to add color to herself. She brushed the rouge over her cheekbones, down to her chin, until the color satisfied herself. She would not look like a frightened child about to be spanked! She added powder lightly, brushed her dark eyebrows with her finger, gazed at the starry wide blue eyes. What did she feel? Panic—excitement—strangeness—incredulity—all those.

Gaylord had gone ahead to the church, leaving detailed instructions behind him. Mara went downstairs with Juana hovering about her, in her best black dress. Enid gazed up at her, and Jennie jumped up and down in bursting delight, as the bride slowly descended the stairs.

"Oh, Auntie Mara, you are like a dream bride," cried Jennie. She hopped on one black slipper, then the other, her rose-pink dress hopping with her.

Enid, in pale blue, smiled approval, then bent to kiss the girl's cheek gently. "My blessings, darling. May you be very happy with Gaylord. He is a good man," she said, with unusual earnestness. "I have never known him to act so impulsively. I know he frightens you at times, but know this, that he does sincerely love you."

Mara lowered her eyelashes. So Gaylord had put on such a good act that he had deceived his own sister! Her mouth tightened. "Thank you, Enid," she said quietly. She turned, glanced up at the landing above. José stood there, quietly, in his dark brown suit melting into the shadows behind him. She looked long at his serious face, then turned away again. He would not be at her wedding, her one true friend, and her heart ached anew.

Lyman Chandler came forward then. "It is time we left for the church, Mara," he said. Fergus was walking beside him, trying to imitate his father's step, his bright eyes unusually animated in his usually placid face. Enid caught at his hand,

and took the two children with her to their carriage. Mara placed her white-gloved hand on Lyman's arm and let him escort her outside, into the wind. The white velvet cloak felt good against the chill.

The drive to the church was silent. Lyman was never a talker, and Mara was too full of her own emotions and confusion. What if she should jump from the carriage and run away? But where could she run? She had no money with her. And Gaylord would only find her and punish her for making him look ridiculous! No, there was no physical escape.

She could only control herself and keep herself aloof from him. He might order her about, she might have to obey him, but it would be rebelliously, sullenly, until he was sick of her!

They came to the church. A small crowd had gathered outside, and good wishes were called in English and Spanish. She recognized several men in the background standing quietly together, their watchful gaze on her face, men she had ridden with in the old days, come to see their comrade-in-arms married. She lifted her chin, gazed at them silently, her veil thrown back, so they could see her face before she turned and went into the church. She was happy they had come. She did not feel quite so deserted. She still had friends, loyal friends, she thought, and some warmth crept into her aching heart.

At the church entrance Enid greeted her, straightened the dress, put down the veil. Jennie reached out and took Mara's hand importantly for a minute.

"Don't worry about anything, Auntie Mara. I'll be walking right ahead of you, and you won't lose your way. This church is very big, but I've been here many times," the small girl whispered.

Enid bit her lips against smiling; Lyman did not seem to hear her. Mara squeezed Jennie's hand and whispered "thank you" gravely.

Then Enid and Fergus went to their places, and the church aisle stretched before Mara. She could hear the music of the immense organ booming through the huge sanctuary. She heard the rustle of the guests as they turned their heads to stare at her. She heard the murmur of the voice of the priest, the singing of the choir above her head and behind her.

Then she was approaching the altar, and her limbs felt stiff and her knees wanted to give way. Gaylord was standing there, turned to watch her approach. He was wearing blue and gold, very tall, very aloof and handsome and strange to her, his face set and watchful.

She began to tremble. Lyman Chandler felt it through his arm and glanced down at her worriedly. At the altar he released her and stepped back behind them. Jennie was close to Mara, but she could not reach out and touch the girl. She stood alone—alone—so alone—

"What am I doing here? Oh, God, why did I let them do this to me?" She stared blindly into the kindly old face of the priest, who was speaking in Spanish and English to them. She was shaking so that her white flowers trembled in her arms.

Behind the cobweb of the white veil she felt faint. It was all unreal, all strange, all a fantasy out of some nightmare. It could not be happening. It was not true. She was alone, so alone. Would she waken, shaking and crying out, to find herself back in the old shadowy house of her youth? When would she waken? When?

Then a hand touched her arm, a strong vibrant hand, and the fingers closed firmly over her wrist. His arm was under hers, and held her up. His voice was speaking firmly; he was so sure of himself! Gaylord's voice, strong, masculine, assured.

He pressed her wrist with his fingers. The priest had turned to her. She lifted her chin and spoke the words in a dream. Answering, committing herself—she sounded loud to herself, but the voice of the priest was louder in her ears. The trembling grew worse; she was shaking uncontrollably. She had never felt so scared, so frightened, so faint.

Gaylord threw back her veil. She had a new ring on her finger beside the blazing sapphire, a ring of gold. Now he gazed down into her face, and his face was strange to her, somehow tender, worried, gentle.

He brushed back the veil further, bent and kissed her mouth gently, his lips pressing softly on her cold mouth. His arm went about her waist, as though to hold her up. Still holding her, he straightened, and they followed the priest to the vestry room to sign the register. Jennie danced after them, holding her flowers daintily, a smile wreathing her face. She had managed it all, she seemed to be saying with her triumphant eyes and her bright smile whenever she saw a familiar face.

Mara could scarcely sign her name, her hand shook so. She managed it finally, and Gaylord took the pen from her. She put her free hand up to her face, brushing it wearily across her eyes. Everything seemed so dark—she swayed.

Gaylord's arm tightened about her. "Come and sit down," he said in her ear, and took her over to a chair. Jennie came to press against her knee, to take her flowers and hold them for her. Enid came to bring her a glass of water. Fergus stood at her elbow gazing gravely at her as his sister held her cold hands.

Gaylord returned. He bent and took her hand in his, chafed it vigorously, as Jennie held the other one. "There, are you better, Mara? I thought you would faint for a moment."

"I am—all right," she said in a whisper.

Jennie kissed her cheek. "I 'spect it was the excitement, Auntie Mara. You have more color now," she said. "Now, we have the reception and food and cake!"

Mara found she could laugh a little as Lyman said, "And the food and cake will be best of all, eh, Jennie? Almost as good as a new dress?"

They went on to the reception, and Mara somehow found strength to greet the whole diplomatic corps who had turned out. She chatted to them in Spanish, English, French, Russian, as though in a dream. Mrs. Desmond came up, and Mara could even smile at her catty face as she said, "I do *hope* you will be very happy, my dear! Remember, do ask me for any advice—"

Mara, answering sweetly, was thinking she would be damned before she did any such thing! The woman went on, and Mara turned to a Russian diplomat, who complimented her on her fine accent in his language.

Gaylord bent to her, to whisper in her ear, "I did not know you spoke so many languages! Truly, I have a prize of a wife!"

He was only teasing, she thought, but his warmth and compliment brought some comfort to her. She smiled faintly. "Thank you. I have always—enjoyed the study—of languages."

"Ah, yes. With the eminent tutor, I believe," said Gaylord, as he straightened to greet the next guest.

Mara bit her lips. How long would José be safe from Gaylord's jealousy? And why was Gaylord jealous? What did she mean to him at all?

Well, in the next weeks and months she would probably find out; she could only hope the learning would not be too painful. If she expected nothing from him, she thought, she could not be too much hurt.

Jennie, pressing against her, caught at her free hand once more and began chafing it in her warm fingers. "It is certainly cold here today," the child remarked, and gazed up at her with wise eyes.

CHAPTER 9

The reception had gone on and on, so that Mara
in her daze thought it might be endless, like a
nightmare run wild. But it was finally over, the
line dissolved, and Gaylord took her in to the
elaborate dinner.

She could eat little. Toasts were drunk, and she
found her champagne glass refilled again and
again. She drank thirstily at first, then more warily as the wine went to her head. But it did warm
her after it reached her stomach. She felt heat,
and the trembling finally stopped.

Gaylord played the loving husband and bride-
groom. She thought "played" because he could
not really mean the tenderness he acted toward
her. He sat close to her, so close that their arms
brushed each other's at the slightest move. He
ordered plates brought to her; she tasted the delicate appetizers, the crisp rolls of bread, the savory
meats, then could eat no more. They cut the huge
white wedding cake, with much laughter from

the guests as Mara handled his huge sword so awkwardly that he had to help her, both arms about her.

She thought of her own delicate blade, the sword she had found in a shop and made her own on her wild adventures during the war. She had handled it skillfully enough! The delicate hilt just fit her hand, the blade was long but slender and slim, sharp as steel could be made.

She wondered if Juana had moved all her possessions to the new room, the trunk of boys' clothing, the caps, the pistols and the sword! What a shock if her husband should ever see those items! They were not typical parts of a bride's trousseau.

Gaylord touched her hand gently, then his warm fingers closed over her cold hand. "Still cold, Mara? Drink this," and he handed her another glass of champagne with his free hand.

She drank again. It did warm her, though it was making her head giddy. He motioned to a waiter, and another plate of hot food was brought, but Mara could scarcely touch it.

Finally he murmured, "We are going now, Mara. I will order your cloak," and she nodded.

It still seemed hours before the coach arrived; she was wrapped in her cloak, and he set her into the closed carriage. They drove away even more slowly, as crowds had jammed the roads near the palace where the reception had taken place. They waved and cheered at the lovely bride and her handsome groom, and Gaylord waved back, smiling. Mara was so weary she felt she could scarcely lift her hand.

She almost went to sleep on the long ride back to La Casa Dorada. The chilled air, the champagne, the warmth of her cloak and the rug over her white lace dress, all combined to make her want to sleep and not waken. Gaylord was silent, and she did not have to think. She could just rest —rest—and not worry—

He put his arm about her waist. "We are home, darling," his deep voice murmured in her ear. "You will be in your own rooms in a few minutes, love. Are you awake?"

She nodded, holding her eyes open with an intense effort. "It was—the champagne," she muttered. "So—sleepy—"

"Of course." Was there a laugh in his voice? The evening dusk had settled down over the golden house and the lovely gardens surrounding it. He helped her out of the coach, lifting her out by her small waist, and setting her gently to the ground. She moved away, too hastily, and stumbled. He caught her and held her. "Wait for me, you will fall!"

He still held her as they went into the huge house. It was oddly silent; the servants were having their own party in the quarters alloted to them. Only the butler was there, dismissing the coach, holding doors for them. Gaylord helped

Mara up the stairs, and they turned to the left toward the new suite.

When they went in Juana got up from the chair. She went to Mara and enfolded her in her tender arms for a moment.

"Ah, my dove, so white and weary! Ah, my little pigeon, here you are. Let Juana take care of my little bird."

Gaylord smiled down at them as the bride drooped wearily into her duenna's arms. "Get her into a comfortable gown and robe, Juana," he ordered. "We will have a tray of food here. She has eaten too little."

He went away to his own room, and Mara thankfully submitted to Juana's tender care. The maid stripped off the white veil, lifted off the white lace dress, unfastened the little white shoes, took off the delicate satin undergarments and slid the cool white satin nightgown over her head. Then she put about her a new white lace negligee, with long wide sleeves that fell to Mara's slim hands, the hands with the new rings. One hand held the blazing blue sapphire and diamond ring and the new gold band. On the other was a huge diamond ring which Gaylord had sent her to wear, two days before, and the diamond bracelet to match.

Juana seated Mara on her chaise longue and began to brush out the blue-black shining curls with a loving touch. Mara relaxed with a deep sigh. She wished she could go to sleep, right here, and not have to waken for a week. Juana was crooning to her, a soft Spanish song, such as she had sung to her as a child. She was so comfortable—if only she could be alone!

A tap on the outer door and Juana scurried to answer it. Mara laid her head down, but the butler brought in a huge tray on a rolling silver table. It was spread with silver and china, steaming plates of hot food under silver covers, and a bucket with more bottles of champagne in it, surrounded with ice.

Mara sighed and sat up again. Gaylord was coming in from his bedroom, looking comfortable but strange to her in his blue and gold dressing gown. He seemed alert, at ease, unweary. She thought resentfully that weddings were easy for him; he did not seem at all tired or perturbed.

While the butler served their plates, Gaylord uncorked the first champagne bottle. He poured out the bubbling golden liquid into two deep-stemmed glasses and handed the chilled glass to her. She took it into her hand, gazing at the bubbles, wrinkling her nose as the bubbles burst against it.

"To us," said Gaylord casually, and touched the glass to his lips. "Drink up, Mara. It will help relax you and get you warm. Are you still cold?"

She nodded. "From my head to my feet. Why are the churches always so cold?" she added plaintively.

"I have heard it is to keep the worshippers awake," he said irreverently, with a laugh. He sat down on a chair opposite her lounge. "Bring a blanket, Juana, and wrap up your white dove. She freezes!"

Juana giggled, brought a white blanket over to Mara, and tucked her up warmly. Mara snuggled down into it and felt much warmer and happier also. Gaylord was so casual, so calm, that she began to feel marriage was not so strange and tense after all.

She was able to eat a little, and Gaylord pressed her to drink more of the champagne. She was dizzy from it, yet more and more it made her feel warm and happy. She leaned her head against the back of the lounge and closed her eyes. If only they would all go away and let her alone, and she could sleep.

The voices around her became more and more dim. She heard the sound of the dishes clinking, the glasses, the champagne cork popping. Gaylord held a glass to her lips. "Drink, little one, just a little more," he coaxed.

She raised her head and drank more, then leaned her head down again. Juana said something in a low disapproving voice; no one answered.

And presently the voices went away, and she was alone. She felt quite comfortable. She muttered a protest when someone lifted her from the warm nest of the white blanket and carried her over to the bed. Someone laid her down and gently removed the white lace negligee. She rolled over into the bedcovers and snuggled down. Now she could sleep—undisturbed—

But someone got into the wide bed with her. Someone big and masculine and hard-feeling drew her into his arms. Gaylord was there, and he would not let her sleep. She muttered and pushed against him, but she was so dizzy, so sleepy.

"It is all right, Mara, it is all right," he whispered in her ears. He drew her against his body, and she felt warm and rather safe there. She put her mussed head against him and snuggled against a warm shoulder. His hand moved through her thick black curly hair and caressed her neck. She wanted to sleep and muttered about that resentfully when he ran his free hand down over her arm.

He chuckled. "So go to sleep," he said whimsically.

"How can I—when you keep—bothering—" she sighed. He ran his hand over her shoulder and down gently to her round white breast. She stiffened, but he just held his hand there and drew her closely to his body. She felt the heat of him all down to his legs. He was so warm, like a stove with an open fire, and she could warm her hands —and her feet—

He kept on bothering her. Just when she was relaxed and used to one caress, he would move his hand, and she would stiffen again warily. But the champagne had made her so dizzy, she could not protest much, and she could not fight him at all. Her limbs felt like water, limp, fluid. When he lifted her arm and put it about his neck, she let it lie there, her hand against the back of his neck, touching the thick blond curly hair.

If she could think, she might be able to fight him, she thought. But she could not think. She could scarcely move of her own volition.

His hands were moving on her again. He lifted the white nightgown, lifted it right off her head and flung it toward the foot of the bed. Then she was as naked as he was, she realized in some surprise. His big hands were busily caressing her all over again.

His mouth moved all over her, following his hands. She could not sleep; she could not protest either. She was dizzy, faint, yet vividly alive, lying limply under his warm body as he moved and did as he pleased with her. His hands—his body —his lips—She could not think of anything but him. Her hands went to his back as he bent to her; she clutched weakly at the hard lean flesh as he moved more rapidly.

Then he hurt her, sharply, and she cried out. His mouth soothed her, his lips on hers, whispering to her softly. He told her it was all right, all right. Then it was better, stranger, not painful now, but—but—what?

Finally he lay back, and she felt the chest under her head moving rapidly as he pulled her over to lie with her cheek against his hairy chest. His hands caressed her smooth back, moving up and down.

"Now—sleep, Mara. You can sleep now, love," he murmured, his voice thick.

Her mind was much involved with all the new sensations. The closeness to a man, the way his hands moved over her, the warmth of his flesh under her cheek, the prickly hairs of his chest. Her fingers clutched at his arm. She was not sure she wanted to sleep. In the dizziness of her mind, she wanted to explore these new sensations, to understand them. But her eyelids were so heavy. She heard him whispering to her, caressing words in English and Spanish.

"Sleep, little dove. Sleep and rest on me, my darling. You belong to me now, you are my own."

She did not understand. He sounded so—loving—so—sweet—so—caressing—She sighed and fell asleep against him.

Sometime in the night she wakened and was suddenly alarmed. Two candles burned on a bedside stand, but the room was strange to her.

She looked about, bewildered, forgetting for a moment all about her marriage, her new rooms, her new life.

She saw the blue satin walls, the thick blue drapes shut against the night. She turned abruptly in the bed and stared down at the man sleeping beside her. When she had sat up, she had disturbed the blankets binding them close together, and the coolness hit his chest, and he opened his eyes. His bright blue eyes gazed up at hers; he was as suddenly awake and alert as though he had not slept.

She brushed back her thick black hair uneasily under his gaze. The movement made her aware of her nakedness, and she stared down at herself. Then Gaylord reached up for her and drew her down to him.

"You are awake, love? Come and be warm," he whispered and drew the blankets up about her once more. His long legs encompassed her small body easily; she was closely held to him. His lips brushed her sleep-warm cheek. His big hand went over and over her back, softly, circling in a little intimate pattern over her shoulders and thighs.

"You looked so startled. Did you find a stranger in your bed?" His lazily teasing voice made her blush in the dim light of the candles.

"I—I wakened, I could not remember—where I w-was," she said.

"Now you remember?"

She did not answer. No answer was necessary. He was causing her to remember—the touch of his hands, his lips, his body, his heat, his passion as it mounted. He turned her, to lie flat on the bed, then he bent over her once more. This time she was not so dizzy that she did not see the wildness flaring in his eyes, the vivid blue of them, the flush of desire on his face. She saw also the lean body bending over hers, before the pressure on her own body made her close her eyes, and feel—feel—so intensely that it seemed every inch of her body was involved in that embrace.

The embrace was long, deliberate, yet always gentle and tender. She was not hurt, she was not startled, he was so deliberately slow, involving her emotions as he roused them with his. This time when he brought them together, she was tense as a bowstring, trembling in his arms, but not with cold. His hands—he was so intimate, so knowing—and his lips, so warm and open on her flesh.

When she drifted off to sleep this time, she was held closely in his arms and had a new knowledge of herself. She knew she was capable of much deeper stranger emotions than she had ever known in her life. She had been close to some knowledge she had not known existed, tantalized by becoming deeply involved—almost—almost close to something—

She slept deeply. She wakened to the touch of

his hands on her face. He was pressing back her hair, studying her face as she had slept. She opened her dazed blue eyes to find his blue eyes so close—

She stared back at him, inches away from her. He smiled.

"Good morning—my wife," he whispered. A hot flush burned over her, flushing her cheeks to wild rose pink. He smiled again, his mouth curving in a more tender look than she had seen from him. "Cannot you answer me?"

She opened her lips, hesitated. Her small tongue licked over her suddenly dry lips. She saw him looking at her mouth, at her tongue. She felt a new person, a woman, shy, strange, lovely, desired. She knew by the look on his face that he was desiring her, and it made her feel hot and uneasy—and happy.

Then, as he moved over her, and his lips pressed to her, she had a sudden cold thought. Gaylord was using her as a man used a woman. He was using her—using her—

A man like her father. A man of many mistresses. They wanted a woman for one purpose only, and this was the purpose.

Yes, he was skillful. Gaylord was an expert in women, Mrs. Desmond had told her that. Now Gaylord was telling her. She thought he was talking in a certain language to her, telling her she

was desirable, that he wanted her. Yes, he knew
this language well.

He spoke this language as her father had spoken it, expertly—to many women. He would use
her until she bored him, until he wanted to talk
that language with some other woman. Then—
she would be discarded as her mother had been,
to weep alone in an empty house, while he stayed
away for years!

Gaylord lifted up, studied her set face, the eyes
that gazed steadily into his. He frowned a little,
obviously puzzled, as her hands lay loosely on the
bed, her arms limp.

"What is it?" he said, half to himself. "What—
what are you thinking, Mara?"

She closed her eyes, to keep the knowledge
from him of how bitter the thoughts were. He
was indeed like her father. She would give him
no weapon to turn against herself. She would
never let him know how he could make her feel,
the delight of his touch, the strange ecstasy that
filled her when he kissed her body. Her pride
would keep her from giving herself away, of betraying herself.

CHAPTER 10

For the next several days Mara moved in a dream.
She felt so strange, as though she had become a
new person, someone she did not recognize.

Her whole life was changed. She had a room
of her own, yet it could be and was invaded at
any moment by a big demanding stranger, who
would come in quietly, or storm in and demand
something.

"Mara, there are guests in the drawing room.
Why are you not dressed? Wear the white with
purple ribbons—quickly, quickly, Juana! It is the
Russian prince, and he brought his wife." And
Gaylord would storm about until Mara was ready
with the appropriate jewelry. Then he would
tuck her hand in his arm and bring her downstairs, to show her off proudly to the visiting
guests.

Or he would come in late at night, when she
was half-asleep, slide into bed with her, turn and
take her into his arms without a word, possessive-

ly, and begin to make love to her as though he owned her.

Which he seemed to do! He owned her every waking and sleeping moment, he seemed to be saying to her. He would touch her with his hands, his lips, and she could not pull away.

Enid had said she would begin to turn over the household to her. "For certainly we shall be returning to England before long, and you must learn how Gaylord likes things managed," said his sister. She showed Mara the accounts, told her about menus and wines, how Gaylord liked things handled. She told her about the households in England, the London town house, the country estate with its huge two-hundred-year-old home, the stables, the land and its farms.

Mara felt completely bewildered by everything. Gaylord had explained nothing to her. She had lived for years in Spain. Did Gaylord expect to leave, to return to England with her? She was not even sure of his work here in Spain. He did work, she knew that now. He spent long hours in his study, over papers, consulting with mysterious guests who came and went from the side doors. He had a full-time male secretary, who seemed to be constantly working with stacks of papers.

Jennie, small and curious, had asked her about the honeymoon and was promptly shushed by Enid. Mara began to wonder about that. Did Gaylord intend to take her on a journey? Where?

When? She dreaded being completely alone with him. Yet—yet—something went thrilling through her at the very thought of having his complete attention for twenty-four hours per day, with no interruptions from visitors or family.

She was seated at her dressing table one morning when Gaylord returned from his room. He had spent the night in her bed, as he usually did, taking for granted that he was welcome, she thought resentfully. She could not call her body her own, or her time. Only her mind and soul remained within her control—to some extent.

He came up behind her at the table. He studied her in the mirror, as she sat with her cup of coffee on the table, with her arms white against the blue satin of the gown, her white throat revealed by the open negligee and nightdress.

"There are several persons arriving this morning, about eleven, for tea, Mara," he said quietly. His hands went to her shoulders, under her clouds of blue-black curls. He lifted them slowly, to circle her throat. He was fully dressed, in his gray silk suit and blue velvet morning jacket, his white cravat tied about his browned throat.

"Oh—yes," she said vaguely, frowning. She had hoped to return to some work, to her studies. She wanted to take refuge in the study of Shakespeare, to have some wall to build up against him. "Is it always—necessary—for me to come down, Gaylord? Surely Enid can greet them. I have nothing in common with—"

"That is not the point, Mara." He said it gently, but very firmly. "You are my wife, my hostess. Enid is showing you how you must act in society. Entertaining is part of the task, and most women eventually find it a pleasant task. I want my friends to be your friends. When we return to England—"

"When is that?" she asked, very quietly, turning tense under his hands.

"Ah—I do not know as yet," he said. He tilted her head back against his shoulder, bent over and kissed her with his face upside-down to hers, his lips clinging to hers. She felt completely helpless, his hands on her throat, held back to his warm body, her mouth captured by his. "Um—sweet," he murmured, and kissed her lips lightly before releasing her. His hands went to her shoulders again, caressing down over her upper arms over the satin. "I think the rose-pink dress today, it will match your cheeks!"

"Gaylord—I wish to ask you questions," she said stubbornly, fighting the weakness in her own body as well as his will. "I thought to remain in Madrid. We have not discussed our future plans. This marriage is a farce—I wish to be released from it! We have not talked about anything; you will not talk seriously to me!"

"Not when you talk like that," he said, his mouth turning hard. She met his frown in the mirror, her gaze was as steady.

"I don't know why you married me," she blurted, her cheeks turning even more pink. "But surely you will let me go now! You have humiliated me, made me obey you. Now, let me go! You may have whatever of the money you want —I don't care. Only let me return to my own home."

His blue eyes flashed flame, but she would not give up the fight. "How dare you speak like that to me!" he roared suddenly. "You insult me! This is your home! You do not understand me at all, you make no effort to do so! You comprehend nothing of the world! You live in a dream world, in a fantasy! No, I will not let you go! I told you —you belonged to me, and I will never let you go!"

She turned his words against him. "Never is a long time, sir!" she said, very coldly. She stood up, facing him, drawing the robe closely about her throat, as though to hide herself from him. "I belong to no one. I am my own person! I will never willingly yield to anyone! You shall never have me, only my body! If that is what you want—I should think you would find other women much more willing, more docile—go and find them!"

He lifted his hand as though to strike her. She did not flinch, glaring at him, her head proudly erect, lifted to his face, as he loomed over her.

He dropped his hand. She was surprised, puzzled by the look that flashed across his face. Pain? Disappointment? Hurt? Rage? She could not understand.

"Mara, you are a child in your comprehensions! Well, I shall have to wait until you mature! But enough of that now. Be ready for our guests —and wear the rose-pink dress!" He turned abruptly and left the room.

She rang for Juana, who brought her breakfast to her. Juana looked into her face, shook her head, and was silent as she ministered to her. She brought the rose-pink undergarments, the rose dress, a rose ribbon for the dark curls, and prepared her for the guests.

When Mara went downstairs, it was to find two of the guests already there, with Enid and Gaylord attentive hosts. Mrs. Desmond and a Spanish lady were there.

Mrs. Desmond was cooing over Gaylord, who sat back lazily in his chair and lapped up her attentions, thought Mara resentfully. Mara deliberately went over to the Spanish lady and began speaking in Spanish to her, so rapidly that no others would follow their conversation. She had known the lady for some years, and they spoke of the war just over, the factions who had fought.

Soon another Spaniard and his wife came in. When he realized what they were discussing, he came over to them as soon as he courteously could, and sat down to enter the conversation animatedly.

"But it would not have been possible to rescue Madrid at that time. It was the only possible move," he was saying in his charming voice, as the other lady and Mara shook their heads. Mara was leaning forward, her face flushed, her hands moving, as she argued with him in quick Spanish, using some of the patois of the south she had learned from her guerrilla friends.

"If only we could have been united in our defiance," she said, when an English voice cut in on their talk.

Mrs. Desmond was drawling, rather loudly, so they would pay attention. "It must be a fascinating topic of conversation, that you should ignore all of us!" she said.

Mara glanced around, the animation dying from her face, something guarded coming. She recognized another Spaniard now, whom she had not seen come in, one of the old enemies. "Merely gossiping," she said in English, with a smile as false as Mrs. Desmond's. "You must excuse us, we have some friends in common. Pardon me," she said in a low tone to the other two, and stood up to leave them.

She went politely to the newcomers, greeted them, aware of her husband's bleak looks at her. Well, he could be absorbed in Mrs. Desmond for an hour! Why could she not talk to her friends? But she realized she had been rude, conversing in Spanish when not all of them spoke it fluently.

She settled down beside a Russian lady she liked and talked to her for a time. Enid was pouring the tea, Jennie was dancing about serving cakes, which she adored doing, as she could listen and hear gossip at the same time. Jennie came over to Mara, her duties done for a moment, and sat down on a stool at Mara's feet. Mara's hand caressed the blonde curly head of Jennie even as she spoke in Russian to the lady. Jennie tugged gently at Mara's skirt, when the Russian lady turned away to speak to Gaylord. Mara bent to her ear.

Jennie whispered, her eyes wide in excitement, "Did you talk about the war to the Spanish people? I heard you say guns and battles and guerrillas!"

Mara stared down at her, wide-eyed. The girl had really learned Spanish if she could catch that. She whispered, "Yes, but it is sort of a secret. We have an enemy here! The man in the red coat—he is not our friend. Don't say anything, Jennie!"

"Ooooh," murmured Jennie, her blue eyes glistening with excitement. "No, I won't, dearest Auntie, I will be quiet. And Mrs. Desmond isn't a friend either, is she? We won't tell her a word!"

"No, don't tell her anything," Mara murmured.

Jennie clasped her small hands together, digesting this great secret. Mara thought, no, Mrs. Desmond was certainly not a friend! Why did she stay, why did she keep coming to see Gaylord? Surely they must have an understanding! Marriage must mean nothing to them. They were—probably—having an affair, an affair of long standing.

She felt surprised that some pain had come with that thought. She must be aware of their relationship. They were so intimate, exchanging looks and smiles and glances. He paid her marked attentions whenever she came. Why had he not married her? Was it the money?

She resolved at another time, soon, very soon, she would offer Gaylord money to release her. It was too humiliating to endure, this marriage to him, when he was fond of Mrs. Desmond. Between affairs with other women, he always returned to Vivienne Desmond; she had assured Mara of that, and Mara believed her. She had seen it happen with her father, when he had a favorite mistress. He would have brief flings with other women, then return to the woman he most admired in those years.

Men were like that, capable of making love to any woman they fancied, she thought. She despised herself, that she had reacted to Gaylord's embraces. She should have held herself aloof, refused to respond, held herself stiff, until he was weary of her!

She was silent during lunch; several of the guests had remained, and she had only to listen and smile and nod and look interested. She was weary of them, of having to look pleasant, when she wanted to run and hide her hurt. She wanted to talk to José; if only she could talk to José!

But Gaylord would be furious with her and take out his anger on José.

After lunch she went up to rest. Juana came to remove her dress and put on her negligee.

"I wish I could talk to José, but I cannot," Mara finally sighed.

"It could be arranged," said Juana quietly, as she had in the old days, when intrigues were planned. The Spanish woman was adept at secrets and meetings and devious thinking. "We could go shopping this afternoon, my dove, down in the heart of Madrid. José could happen to be at a café where we pause for our coffee. Would that not do?"

"Oh—yes, yes, Juana. Do plan that, but do not let any trouble arise about it! If José thinks it is not safe—"

"Do not worry, my dove. Would I let you get into difficulty with anyone?" Juana smiled, and brushed out her blue-black hair with soothing touch.

Comforted, Mara rested, and then got up early to dress in a warm blue velvet dress and the black velvet cloak she liked for nighttime rendezvous.

She could not wear her rusty black gowns any more; they were all burned, but this would hide her dress, and the hood would hide her face and hair.

They took a closed carriage and went shopping. Mara and Juana were both on edge, watching the time. Mara bought a handbag and shoes she did not need, then impatiently ordered the carriage to the café.

"It is early, my dove," Juana warned.

"José is always early. And I do so wish to talk to him." She turned her head and thought she recognized a man across the street. A warning flashed automatically to her brain. "Was that one of the men who—"

"Who, my dove?" Juana turned her graying head alertly, but the man had vanished.

"Nothing. I am seeing ghosts of the past. I wonder if the hate will always linger, the hates from the wars. But they must linger—because of the uncertainties of the present growing out of the past. Why could the men not have formed a new government, made a fresh start, instead of trying to rebuild the monarchy? We know what the king was, a weakling, a traitor—"

"Hush, my dove, it is not safe to say such things," whispered Juana. "And who else was there?"

"No one—but the unknowns. They might have

worked, with more skill, with the support of the people—but José says—"

They entered the closed carriage and started toward the street of the café where they meant to rendezvous with José. They reached the street, the carriage paused. Juana got out and turned to wait for Mara as the coachman stepped down. He was wearing the distinctive uniform of Gaylord's men, blue and gold, with the crest on his uniform matching the crest on the carriage.

He reached up to help Mara down. She saw José at the back table and sent a tiny smile toward him as she put her foot out to step down.

But two men dashed up. One knocked Juana down, and the older woman rolled helplessly on the walk near the café tables. The other knocked out the coachman with a blow from behind. Then the second man, pushing Mara back into the closed carriage, slammed the door after him as he jumped in.

She fell back against the soft cushions, gasping. She saw José jumping up, running, as another man began to run after him. She began to fight the man in the carriage, but he was huge, strong, his face scarred. She knew that face; she had met him before.

He was one of the men who followed Lope Sanchez-Garcia!

She fought him in silence, viciously, kicking

out, scratching, biting, with her fingernails as weapons. She cursed herself for not having a pistol or weapon of any sort.

The carriage started up with a jerk which caused Mara to fall back against the cushions again. The man pinned her down, and with one hand he wrapped a scarf about her head, gagging her. When he had that secure, he held her in his arms, hatefully, grinning down at her as she fought against the cloak and his arms.

"You might as well lie still, wildcat," he said thickly, in Spanish. "You are fairly caught, and you have none of your men to rescue you this time! And no horse to carry you off!"

She was out of breath, mussed, frightened, hot in the cloak, furious at being held in that way. But back of her fury was fear—

For they had often threatened to catch her alone and torture her for what she had done. And now that she was off guard, thinking the wars over and done, it had happened.

They had captured her. Her enemies had her at last, and they would be merciless. She had beaten them too often in the past, and she had killed.

Now it was their turn. And who would come to her aid? José was weak, alone, helpless. Her men had disbanded, and they had their own families, their own futures to consider. They were older, settled, with more at stake than when they had been restless foot-loose young daredevils.

For a few moments she thought of her men, how they might rage when they heard of her torture and death. She grimaced. It would be too late to help her then!

Her thoughts turned wistfully to Gaylord. What if she had married a daring young man, who had truly adored her, loved her deeply. Would he then have come to her rescue?

But she was a practical woman dealing with things as they were. Gaylord had married her for his own reasons, probably her money. From all appearances he was still attracted to Vivienne Desmond.

No, she could expect no help from him. No help from anyone. She would have to rescue herself— if she could.

Her mind began working busily on various possibilities.

CHAPTER 11

She stopped struggling, wanting to save her energy and wits for the encounter with Lope Sanchez-Garcia. Her captor seemed to recognize that she had surrendered for the moment, and he loosened his grip on her, though he sat watchfully at her side, ready to grab her.

They rode for a long time, out into the countryside. Mara realized they were taking her to the country home of Sanchez-Garcia, probably so they could feel free to torture her! She remembered the torture instruments in the basement of his home, the dark cellars filled with wine casks and instruments from the Inquisition, and shuddered. She prayed briefly for strength to endure whatever might happen to her, and a swift death if the agony was too great.

But she was too vital, too alive, and courageous to dwell long on that. She was not dead yet; she was not even injured. And she had her wits about her. They had rescued her in the past, they could again.

By the time they had reached the country home, she was in command of herself and had a plan which she thought might work. After all, Lope Sanchez-Garcia was in a precarious position politically. He dared go only so far. His fury might drive him, but he had caution also, and she would play on that.

The carriage was driven up to a side door, and several men promptly surrounded it. She was escorted into the house by several armed men and hid a smile. After all, she did have a reputation! She raised her head proudly and flung back the hood of the black velvet cloak as she entered.

Her first captor escorted her to a back drawing room. There Lope Sanchez-Garcia rose when she entered. His black eyes were narrowed and cold.

"So—you got the female," he said in Spanish. His merciless eyes roamed over Mara as the cloak was removed, and she stood there in the close-fitting, graceful, and very feminine blue velvet dress. "You look much more the woman than you used to! But underneath is the same cruel wildcat, eh? Well, the cat will be tamed! There is only one way to treat a killer panther!"

She was silent, watchful, as he walked around her and issued several curt commands in Spanish. Then he returned to her, and with mockingly polite courtesy, invited her to a seat. She chose a straight chair and sat down, her back erect, her eyes narrowed to study his expression.

He went back to his tall stiff Spanish armchair and sat down, very much the Spanish aristocrat. But she remembered his reputation. He was no gentleman, but a traitor, a coward, one who played both sides and chose the one who paid him most.

"Yes, yes," he said, as though to himself, but he meant to make her listen. "You are much more attractive than I had thought! You have become beautiful, eh? You are like a lady, eh? Only beneath is the same peasant killer, the same boyish female who rode with the guerrillas, and betrayed, and killed!"

"I killed, yes. But never betrayed," she was stung into retorting. "That was your role, Sanchez-Garcia!"

His eyes narrowed, and she took a fresh grip on her temper. "It was none of your battle. You should have stayed out of our family matters! We Spanish do not take kindly to outsiders!"

She bit her tongue against saying how they had bowed down to Napoleon and his followers. She listened, her slim hands lying quietly in her lap. She noted his gaze on her, the bold intimacy roving over her body, back to her face and hair. She caught her breath at his insolence as he leaned forward to study her face more closely, blowing cigar smoke into her eyes.

"Yes, yes, quite pretty now," he said mockingly. "Cristobal used to say you would become a beauty. But I could not believe him as I saw you in those thick black dresses. A disguise, yes? As the boyish clothing was a disguise. Your husband will miss you—for a short time—before Vivienne Desmond comforts him, eh?"

She kept her face smooth; her blood was up at the challenge before her. She meant to keep herself alive. She must be cunning, daring, imaginative, deadly.

"You do well to remember my husband, señor," she drawled in Spanish. "He is an Englishman, Viscount Kelton. He is here on an official matter of the British crown. Who touches his wife, touches him, and that touches the King of England. You would do well to consider the matter."

A flicker in the black eyes told her the shot had gone home. She was silent then, not pressing it. He was uneasy, his fury checking.

He crossed his legs, scowled, finally got up abruptly and left the room, leaving only a guard inside the room with her. The man stood silently, watchfully, near the door.

She did not let herself relax, except to ease her taut muscles, ready for whatever might come. On the wall she saw some huge swords, but they

were too high for her to reach. Still—a chair—
the sword in her grip. She could manage a large
sword for a short time. Pistols? Her alert gaze
roamed the room, saw none. But the desk there
might hold a brace. If the guard dozed, or was
called away—

But she was alone only an hour or so, and then
her captor returned.

He had several men with him, his servants by
the looks of them. Two had their coats off, sleeves
rolled up.

"Come. We will go to the cellars. I have some
questions to ask of you, and I believe you will
answer more readily there. Come!" And he grabbed
her arm and brought her to her feet.

She knew he meant torture and replied quietly. "Again, I will ask you to consider carefully
what this will mean. If the wife of an English viscount is murdered—"

"Who says murder? You merely disappear.
Who saw you go? No one but your duenna. Who
will believe the old woman? And your husband
will be glad to be rid of a wildcat of a wife, who
was wealthy in the bargain," the man jibed, and
laughed at the rich color that came to her cheeks.

Yes, he might be glad to be rid of her, she
thought. Then, unaccountably, she remembered
Gaylord's tenderness of last night, as he had lain
in her bed with her in his arms. The way his big
hands had roamed over her body, the way he had

bent over her and caressed her silken skin, whispering to her in Spanish and English, passionately, until she too was swept up with his passion and had begun to respond to him.

They were now in the hallway, when there was a pounding at the huge front door. Mara started, her nerves on edge, and noted that her captor was nervous also. "Send them away, whoever it is," he barked at one of the men. The man rushed to the front door.

As he opened it their little group paused. The door opened a crack—then burst open to full extent as a seeming crowd of men stormed in.

Gaylord was in the front, behind him José. Gaylord saw Mara at once and stalked past the servant back through the hallway to them. His eyes were blazing bright blue, his face drawn and furious with rage.

"Why do you have my wife here?" he asked slowly, in a deadly cold voice.

Lope Sanchez-Garcia began to stammer.

Mara cut in. "He captured me. He was just dragging me to the cellars to torture and question me."

The words fell into a short silence. José had come to range himself beside Gaylord. The tall Britisher was weaponless, but José had a small sword in his hand, held casually, but effectively. Behind them were the guardsman, Ramón Olivera, and two others from Gaylord's stables, big and burly and somehow very reassuring.

"Your explanation, señor?" Gaylord was coldly polite. "And release my wife!" He held out his hand imperiously. Lope started and let Mara go. She went over slowly to Gaylord, careful not to step between the two men. "You think to capture the wife of a British diplomat? I wonder at your daring—or is it madness?"

Lope Sanchez-Garcia seemed to have recovered his poise. He had the nerve of a snake, Mara thought.

"If you will step into my drawing room, señor," he gestured to them, "I think my explanation will satisfy you! Indeed, I think you may be grateful to me for revealing the extent of the misdeeds of your—wife—" And he walked in front of them into the drawing room.

Gaylord took Mara's cold hand in his, his bright blue eyes seeming to flash over her, as though questioning, reassuring all at once. She was in a daze. She had been so sure that no one would rescue her, no one would come. But *he* had come, her guardian, her enemy, her husband, her demanding, dominating, infuriating tender man.

They went inside and stood, though the host tried to get them to be seated.

"I want merely a simple explanation of your actions, señor," said Gaylord again, holding Mara's hand tightly. "You dared to strike her duenna, carry her off in my own carriage! You brought

her here, and she tells me you meant to torture
and question her. Why? How dare you touch her?"

"I dare—because of what she is," said the
Spaniard. José stood close behind Mara, so close
she could have touched him, and she felt his tension. Almost as though she could see his mind,
she felt him thinking, figuring, planning.

"You would do better," drawled Gaylord coldly,
"to consider what I am! I am a soldier, trained in
battle. I am a Britisher, trained for the diplomatic
corps, but also for fighting. Do you think I am incapable of protecting my own? And this lady belongs to me. She was my ward, as the daughter of
an old friend. She is now my wife. Do you think
I would abandon her?"

"If you truly knew her, you would!" The Spaniard's black eyes gleamed with threat. "She is a
bitch. She has as her lover that dog there—" And
he pointed directly at José. "The two of them
rode the countryside together, she in boys' clothing, during the war. They fought, betrayed, killed,
together! They carried information, had their fellow Spaniards murdered! They themselves killed.
He carries a wound in him which I myself in-
flicted! She—but for her luck—she would be a
dead dog of a spy! She and her lover—"

"Enough!" Gaylord's voice had turned curt and
rough. His grip tightened cruelly on Mara's hand.
"You will not abuse my wife to me!"

"She is a bitch! You will soon discover it for

yourself. Do you want another man's leavings?"

Gaylord dropped Mara's hand. Like lightning, he flashed out and snatched the small sword from José's hand. "No," cried Mara. "No, no, no—"

But Gaylord was lunging at Lope. Lope had snatched a sword from the wall and was leaping forward, satanic joy on his dark face. His sword was longer, he had a better reach. Gaylord would not have a chance—

"Give me a sword, I will fight him myself!" screamed Mara, beside herself with fury. "Give me a sword—I will kill that dog, that pig—!"

But her husband had lunged forward to meet Lope's attack. The short sword was no match for the long one, but Gaylord parried the attack, fended it off. His eyes were narrowed, keen. He lunged past the guard, managed to prick Lope's coat. The Spaniard leaped back, then holding the sword before him, he moved slowly forward. The other men stepped back to allow them room. José pulled Mara with him, muttering in her ear. "Do not distract them, Mara. Do not—he has a chance—"

"This is for my Cristobal!" cried Lope, and lunged forward. "She gave the order for his death! I will kill you—and then her! She shall pay, and pay dearly—" And his sword pricked at the sleeve of Gaylord's coat, ripping it open.

Mara gasped and would have dashed forward, but that José was holding her tightly by both arms.

"No, no, no," he muttered to her. "Do not, Mara, do not distract—"

She watched Gaylord's face, then his enemy's, in an agony of apprehension. She felt tight, drawn, frightened as she had never been for herself. They were not matched fairly. If only Gaylord had a longer sword—she recognized his superior skill with the sword. But two things were against him—the short sword—and his fury.

He was being drawn on to lunge. Lope was muttering taunts, in English now, his black eyes watchful, cold, cruel. "She is a bitch, your wife! She rode with men. She slept with them. She was notorious throughout Spain. All Spain laughed when you married her—and in white lace! Bah, she is no good, that one!"

Gaylord rushed forward, was met by the point of the sword. Mara screamed, as the sword seemed to go right through his right side. The coat was ripped—his side turned to a mass of blood—he stood, swayed—

Lope pulled out the sword and laughed as the other man fell. Mara rushed to him, pulling herself from José, and knelt beside her husband. She moved back the coat with trembling hands and pressed her scarf to his side. The blood was spurting from his side. "Oh—God—God—my God—" she whispered in an agony.

"Get up, woman, bitch!" Lope yelled at her, and his sword pricked at her shoulder. "Take his sword! If you wish to fight, you shall! But you shall die too!"

She did not spare a glance for him. She was frantically ripping at Gaylord's white lawn shirt, to open it to the wound. The blood, the blood on her hands—she must stop the blood from spurting.

In a daze she heard José's cool tones in Spanish. "Calmly, more calmly, señor. You do not consider. You have done a grave error. Let us consider it. You must not go further. Let us go, and take the Englishman to his home. If he recovers, you may not be charged by the police. We might keep it quiet."

"I would kill the woman, the bitch," the other man was yelling.

"I think not," said José, quite calmly, reflectively. Mara spared a brief glance upward, to see the two men squared off, the older man with his bloody sword, José with only his two brown eloquent hands. "You see, the situation is thus, señor," drawled the tutor in professorial tones. "You have gravely wounded a British diplomat after carrying off his wife. Your position here in Spain is already precarious. If the scandal is known, if you kill, and kill again, you are finished in Spain. All your careful maneuvers to return to power will topple you down—down—to nothing."

Gaylord's bright blue eyes were open; he was gazing upward at the two men, even as Mara and Ramón Olivera worked over him, trying to stem the flow of blood. He was listening, she was sure of that.

José talked on and on, slowly, calmingly, persuasively. He told the other man how he would be ruined by this rashness, how he would accomplish nothing but his own downfall. All his efforts of the past years would be as nothing, he would be exiled from his own country, from his Spain. He would lose his home, his houses, they would be taken by the state. "And what a pity, señor, your house of four hundred years ownership, the house your ancestors built—with no one to occupy them, gone to strangers. No chance for you to marry and leave them to your sons."

How eloquent, how clever was this José, thought Mara, feeling some distant amusement, even as she bent over her husband and tied the bandage tightly about his waist. He would persuade the devil himself; indeed, that was what he was doing now!

"Oh, very well, take him away! But beware of me," growled Sanchez-Garcia reluctantly. "If he lives, I shall ruin him in other ways. All Spain shall know of his wife and her past life! Her amours shall be notorious, as she is!"

Mara felt Gaylord give a convulsive move of anger, as though he would jump up. She held him warningly, and at her nod Ramón Olivera held him gently back in his strong arms. The young guardsman could be a strength, thought

Mara, and gave him a grateful smile.

Somehow José had soothed Sanchez-Garcia, and the man let them go. Ramón and another man carried him out to the darkened carriage, and Mara got in with him, to hold him on the return trip to La Casa Dorada. José got in also, to crouch on the floor, and try to hold Gaylord steady as the carriage jolted on the rough roads.

It was a nightmare journey, for Gaylord became unconscious sometime on the way, and Mara thought he might be dead. Dead, all because he had come to her rescue—as she had not even dreamed that he would!

How strange life was, more like a dream, she thought. A dream—in which nothing was the way she thought it was. Here, instead of being tortured to death in the cellars of her enemy, she was sitting, unharmed, in a carriage, holding Gaylord—wounded, unconscious. And he did not love her, she was certain of that. Why had he come?

CHAPTER 12

When the carriage with the wounded man returned to La Casa Dorada, Enid screamed, fainted, and was no use at all. Her husband was occupied in caring for her.

Only José and Gaylord's valet were any good at all. Mara sent for a British doctor who could be trusted to hold his tongue, then set to work to stem the fresh spurts of blood. José and Juana brought bandages, hot water, cold water, medicines. Juana kept wringing her hands, moaning that the lord was dead.

José helped Mara fasten the bandages tightly, soothed Mara when a fresh spurt of blood upset her. "Calmly now, Mara, calmly, I have seen worse wounds than his. And he is a strong young man in good health. Calmly now; you cannot aid him if you are weeping like Juana! Where is your good sense, my child?"

"I never dreamed he would come after me," said Mara, bending over the unconscious man.

She scarcely knew what she was saying. "I am guilty of his death! If I had not been so careless, I should have been on guard—"

José gave her a sharp glance, his eyes narrowed. "Ah, who can predict what such a one as that Sanchez-Garcia will do?"

"Any man of such adoration would come after his wife!" Juana exclaimed through her tears. "Ah, he loves you, my little señora, my little dove, he adores you! Of course he would come to your rescue, flying there. Such a rage he went into when José returned and informed him of your danger! I thought he had run mad! Such fury, such anger —ah, if any man thought so of me, I would marry him at once, I tell you!"

Mara frowned down at her husband, unconscious on his huge bed. Love? No, more likely his pride, that anyone should take any piece of his property from him!

The doctor arrived, and Lyman Chandler left his distracted weeping wife long enough to impress on him the importance of keeping the matter a secret.

"For he is on a delicate mission. We must put out that he is stricken gravely ill of an unknown disease and cannot receive visitors. It cannot be known that he has fought a duel with a Spaniard, a member of our host country!"

Mara was puzzled, but she and José kept silent. She was still in the dark about Gaylord's mission to Spain. She had thought it was only social duties, until just recently, when she realized he had graver matters on his mind.

The British doctor promised discretion, warning however that he must report it to the embassy. He gave complete instructions on how Gaylord was to be cared for, treated him efficiently, and promised to return in the morning to check on his progress.

Mara changed to her nightgown and robe and came back anxiously to her husband's room. He was semiconscious, his eyes sometimes opening to survey the room vacantly. He was feverish and hot and kept throwing off his covers.

She tucked the blankets about him again. The valet whispered that he would remain awake and tend him. Mara shook her head.

"I will stay with him tonight. You get some sleep and be prepared to care for him in the morning," she murmured. The man finally bowed and went to his room nearby.

The room was cool, as it was winter now, and the Spanish nights could be cold. Mara found another blanket and put it about her, as she sat in the large armchair near his bed. To keep herself awake, she studied his face, his hands. He was so tanned, so strong, it seemed impossible that one moment had laid him low, had gravely injured him. He could have been killed; he might yet die!

And she—how would she feel? Guilty, she

thought. Very guilty, that her past had caught up with her and involved him! She had never meant to harm anyone else by her secret past. She had thought it was over and done.

And Gaylord—he had come for her. Why? Why? She reached over timidly to touch his strong brown hand. To her shock, the hand turned and clasped hers strongly. "Mara," he muttered.

She held her breath.

"Mara!" he said again, and opened his eyes. The bright blue gaze was feverish. He turned his head to look at her. "Mara?"

"Yes, yes, I am right here," she murmured. She left the chair to come and sit gently on the side of the bed near his left side, studying his face anxiously. He clung to her hand firmly. She let her fingers curl about his long fingers. She pressed his hand. "Do you not feel I am here?"

"Mara," he said again, and closed his eyes. She did not know if he knew what he was saying; she thought not. She curled up on the bed patiently, to wait until he became conscious again. Then because she was cramped and chilled, she finally pulled the blanket over to her and snuggled down at his side to wait for him to waken once more.

"Mara?" The voice roused her from half-sleep. She sat up, her hand still in his.

"Yes, I am here," she murmured.

"I am—dry—mouth—dry—" he muttered. His

lips seemed parched, feverish.

The doctor had said he could have a little water mixed with wine. She reached over to the bedside table and poured out a little wine into a glass, then added water. She put her hand under his head, surprised to find it so heavy, and half-raised him to take the wine.

He sipped at it, then lay back with a sigh. His half-opened eyes opened wider, studying her, as though puzzled to find her there. "Mara—missing? Were you—gone—"

"Yes, but you found me and came for me," she said softly. She was not over the miracle of it, that he had come for her, that he had cared—for some reason—to come for her.

"Found you. That damn villain—" His voice was a little stronger in his anger.

"Yes, yes, but that is over. You are here. Lie quietly, for you were wounded." He seemed restless, and she timidly stroked his forehead. Her touch seemed to soothe him, and she went on stroking, brushing back the thick blond hair from his forehead, moving her palm slowly down over his tanned cheek, to his chin and lips, back around the other side. His eyes closed. He lay without moving while she touched him.

He slept again, his breathing more even. Cautiously she lay down with him, curled up at his side, and tried to stay awake. She dozed off again and again, but wakened alertly whenever he moved. She gave him wine and water twice more in the night.

Finally it was morning, and the sunlight was creeping between the folds of the drawn drapes. She got up stiffly, and went to open the drapes and let in the warmth and light. When she returned to the bed, he was awake, his blue eyes gazing up at her.

"The sunlight—your house was so dark—" he muttered. She thought he was still feverish.

She stroked his forehead gently. "Yes, my house —was always so dark. I love the warmth, the light of La Casa Dorada," she said in a gentle soothing monotone.

"You like—my house—our house—" he whispered. His head turned restlessly as soon as her hand left him. She put her palm against his cheek, and at once he was quiet again.

"Yes, it is so beautiful," and she sat down on the side of the bed and talked to him slowly. "The sunlight shines on the polished floors, on the beautiful bright rugs. It is like life after death to come here, it is so beautiful and bright and sunny. It is—as though I lived—for the first time—in my life. I like to walk in the gardens, among the flowers, and hear the fountains playing. The little dolphins and laughing cupids are so gay and pretty."

She was talking only to soothe him, scarcely

knowing what she said. A half-smile touched his lips. She held a glass to his lips; he drank and lay back again. She went on talking, in a sort of rambling monologue, until his eyelids drooped and shut, opened, shut again, and stayed closed.

Finally the valet came in. She stood up wearily as the man silently took her place beside the bed. She whispered instructions to him, telling him to call her at once if she were needed. Then she went back to her bedroom.

Juana was coming in with a tray of breakfast; hot coffee, hot rolls, honey, eggs. Mara ate and drank in a daze, then fell into her own bed to sleep hard.

She felt as though she had slept only a moment, when Juana's hand was on her shoulder, wakening her.

"My lord is calling for you, little dove. He wants you, will you come, love?" her maid was saying.

Mara rolled out of bed, reached for her negligee, and put her feet into her slippers. She padded into the next room. Gaylord was half-sitting up, his head turning restlessly, muttering feverishly. Sunlight blazed into the room, which was hot and airless.

Mara went to the curtains, drew them. It must be late afternoon. She opened the windows slightly, so that fresh air and coolness of the winter afternoon came in. Then she returned to the bed.

"Did the doctor come this morning?" she asked the valet.

"Yes, my lady. He came and said he would return this evening. My lord is very feverish, the wound may be infected," the valet murmured anxiously.

Mara nodded, her mouth tight. She had feared this. She turned back the covers. Gaylord was staring at her with bright unseeing eyes. Gently she turned back the edge of the bandage, to find the wound bleeding and red about the edges. The valet brought cool water; she bathed about the side, not near the wound, but just to it. Gaylord's muttering subsided. She removed two of the blankets and gave him some water and wine to drink.

"He has had nothing to eat?" she whispered.

"No, nothing, my lady."

"Ask for hot broth and sops. I will try to get him to eat just a little, or he will lose all his strength."

The valet nodded, seemingly relieved to have someone in command. He returned presently with a silver bowl and cover on a tray. Lyman Chandler arrived with him and bent over his brother-in-law with a troubled look.

"Doesn't look good," he muttered.

"He has lived these first hours," said Mara, more calmly than she felt. "He has every chance now." She sat down on the bed and dipped a piece of soft bread into the broth. She put it to

Gaylord's mouth. He turned his head away restlessly. "Yes, eat, please. Gaylord? Eat, just a little piece."

He opened his mouth, and she popped it inside. She spooned more broth into his mouth, he swallowed, as though his mouth and throat were dry and hard. But he did eat and drink, and she was pleased. When he would eat no more, she laid aside the bowl, and put her hand to his forehead.

"He is more cool now," she murmured. "That is good. I will stay with him a time."

"But you must eat also, Mara," said Lyman Chandler gravely, looking down at her from his height. "Come down to dinner with us. Enid will be reassured."

She shook her head. "No, I will stay with him," she said firmly. "Tell Enid he is recovering nicely. And warn the children not to speak of this. They are sure to have heard the full story."

Lyman grimaced. "Oh, yes, they have all the details from Ramón Olivera. That young man— he must not talk! But of course those monkeys of mine are adept at worming information from anyone. And listening at keyholes! I caught Jennie at my study the other morning!"

When Gaylord seemed easier, Mara went to bathe and dress. Juana helped her, murmuring prayers automatically for the health of the lord. Mara found herself echoing them in her heart, for she was more anxious than she had revealed to Lyman.

The doctor came in the evening and found her sitting quietly beside the bed.

"Ah, yes, he does seem better," he said, more cheerfully. "Do you understand what I am saying, my lord?" he added, as Gaylord opened his eyes following the examination.

"Right, and you are hurting me damnably," said Gaylord feebly, with a grimace.

"Well, well, you are recovering then, if you can swear," and the doctor laughed. "Your loving wife has taken good care of you. Your man tells me she sat up all night with you."

The blue gaze turned to Mara's face. She half shut her eyes against its intensity; he seemed to look right through her. Loving wife? The words had sent a shock through her. Yes, she did love him. Unwillingly, reluctantly, she had come to love him, this dominating, strong, bullying man who had forced her to marry him, who had taken her from a house of shadows and past, to a house of sunlight and future that she was unhappy about facing.

She stayed up with Gaylord that night also, but he was better and did not need such close attention. She half-slept in the big chair until about midnight when he wakened.

He was dry and parched again. She set the cool wine and water to his lips, and he drank.

"But you are not resting, Mara," he said finally, and sounded like his old authoritative self. "Lie down with me and get some sleep, if you must remain!"

She flushed. It sounded as though he did not want her. "I sent the valet to sleep," she said defensively. "And you should not be alone."

"Come here, then," he said, and held out his left arm to her. She frowned, hesitated. "Come here, Mara!"

She came and lay down on top of the covers beside him. "No, that won't do, you are uncomfortable. Get inside the covers," he ordered. He seemed about to haul her around.

"Don't move, Gaylord, please! You will open the wound and it is just beginning to heal!" She sat up.

"Then do what I tell you and don't cause me any difficulties!" His mouth was amused, his blue eyes teasing.

She crawled under the covers, beside him, holding herself aloof from him. Now that she knew she loved him, it was half-pain to be so near him. She feared betraying herself, letting him know that she had fallen victim to his charm, the same charm her father had used so devastatingly.

When she wakened later, she found herself with her head on his shoulder, his arm about her. But he was lying quietly, sleeping, so she did not move to disturb him. She held her breath, her lips

so near his throat she could have kissed him. She
wondered dreamily how it would feel to be loved
by him as she loved. Would he welcome her caresses then? Would he lie still, his eyes half-shut,
his mouth tender, as she bent over, and just—
touched—his throat—with her lips?

But she must not think about this. He did not
love her; he wanted only to conquer her and
make her do as he said. She would be lost if she
loved, for then he would discard her. This way, if
she did not reveal her love, she might lie often in
his arms, being held by him, hugged, caressed,
his hands roaming over her, feeling his tenderness,
his passion as he desired her.

Only she must not respond—must not—

She fell asleep on that resolve.

He was better in the morning and insisted that
she must rest. She slept in her own room and in
the afternoon returned to find him sitting up chatting with the doctor.

"He is making an excellent recovery," the doctor said cheerfully. "Only you must persuade him
not to leave his bed, my lady! I want him to remain in bed at least a week or perhaps ten days.
The wound must be given a chance to heal. And I
want no visitors flocking in to disturb him!"

Gaylord only smiled. After the doctor left, he
said quietly to Mara, who was alone with him,
"Now I would like some answers to my questions,
Mara."

His eyes were sharp and keen, his mouth stern. He indicated the chair beside the bed, and she went reluctantly to seat herself there. Her hands folded tightly onto each other, and he did not miss the movement as she symbolically shut herself against him.

"I think you should not overtire yourself," she said.

"That is up to you. I wish to hear the full story of all you did in those years you lived alone in Madrid."

"I—I lived with my father," she protested, weakly.

His eyes narrowed. "I think not. I think he had no idea of what you were doing. Now, your story, Mara. You spied, I think? With José?"

Her mouth compressed. He questioned her again and again, more sharply, as she was reluctant to tell him. Finally she submitted a little.

"Well, well, I will tell you something! Only you realize I am putting our lives in your hands!" she said angrily, with a toss of her blue-black hair. "If anyone hears of this, if they know the full extent of how we spied for Wellington, who rode with us—no, I cannot tell you all that!"

"You will tell me everything!" he said sternly. "I am your husband, and I have a right to know."

She lifted her chin. "It is not entirely my secret," she said firmly. "I will not betray my friends! Only know this, that José and I were partners, never lovers. We spied for the sake of Spain, for honor, for patriotism, to protect the innocent. We rode—to give information to Wellington, so that the French could not overrun the country!"

"Tell me," he insisted, his gaze sharply on her face. "And I thought you were a rusty little spinster, too old for her years, in a plump black dress! God! Go on, Mara!"

She told him reluctantly, cautiously, some of the facts. How she and José had ridden with their information, how they had listened at receptions, how he had learned of troop movements and the stationing of officers. How they had heard of traitors. She told of Cristobal and Lope Sanchez-Garcia, their part in villainy, how they rode with one side and accepted money from the French to betray their own fellow Spaniards.

"And Cristobal was the worst," she said grimly, carried away with her story. Her eyes glowed with fury. "We found him, the gold in his pockets, our comrade hanging in the wind! We took him, and Lope followed. We made Lope stand in his ropes, straining against them, while we tried Cristobal and sentenced him to death for his greed and betrayal!"

"And you, Mara, you sentenced him—" Gaylord asked very gently.

"Yes, I!" Her chin was up proudly. "I fought with them, I commanded them at times. They ac-

cepted my leadership! Then later, when José was
injured—"

He made her tell him of that incident, how
they had been surrounded, captured. How José
had been shot. She had taken his pistol as well as
her own, had killed a man, wounded another, had
been stripped of weapons down to her sword,
with no time to reload the pistols. "So I fought
my way free, señor, and dragged José to the horse
with me, and we got away."

"You are—a gallant fighter, Mara," he said
quietly. "But I do not want you fighting any
longer! You are married to me, and I will not have
it! If there is any fighting to do, I shall do it for
you! It is my right!"

She frowned at him. "The wars are over, señor,"
she said curtly. "Only those like Sanchez-Garcia
do not forget. I may have to defend my own life
at times!"

"Not while I am here," he said firmly. Her eyes
went to her clenched hands. What did he mean?
That he might leave her? That he might desert
her as her father had deserted her mother? A
wave of such keen anguish swept over her, that
it quite frightened her. Oh, she did not want to
love! It hurt to love. It made her furious and
heartsick to love!

She would not tell him any more of her story.
Reluctantly, he let her go for then, but kept ques-

tioning her from time to time. She was glad to let Enid sit with him and entertain him. And presently as the days passed, he was strong enough to sit in the winter garden, blankets about him, to recover in the beautiful sunlight.

One afternoon, wearing a white muslin dress with a black cloak over it, she went to gather some roses. She had seen a few left in the shelter of a pavilion. As she went near the place, she realized it was occupied. Enid was there—with Ramón Olivera.

Mara sighed and frowned. She had hoped the little romance had run its pace and was over. Enid was quite aware that Mara knew of it, but still she kept on.

Mara retreated and went to find Gaylord. It would not do for him to discover his sister. She found him sitting in a chair.

"I wonder that you come to me now," he said without greeting, scowling up at her.

She gazed down at him wide-eyed. He had not spoken so coldly and angrily to her in weeks. "What is it? Gaylord, are you ill?"

"No, but I saw you just now. Going to the pavilion to meet that Ramón Olivera, the guardsman. Yes, I recognized your dress and your cloak, and you are wearing them even yet! You have been with him quite an hour. How dare you? How dare you flaunt your affair in my face? Do you think I am blind as well as injured? I thought you loved José, but you have convinced me you are merely close friends. However, this affair with Ramón—I will not endure it!"

He was working himself into a rage. Mara sighed deeply. She could not betray his sister, Enid. Her code of honor had been strongly developed during the war. What could she say, what could she do?

He was an intensely jealous and possessive man. He knew little of her, and he was curious about her.

"I will tell you this," Mara, quietly, managed to interrupt him. "I do not love Ramón. I feel nothing for him. He is a fine young man, and a good guardsman, of a fine family. But I do not love him. No matter what appearances say, I do not."

"Then why do you meet him secretly?" asked Gaylord, and there were high spots of color in his cheeks, as when he was feverish.

"I cannot tell you," said Mara, and would not discuss it further. Gaylord was furious with her, scarcely speaking to her the remainder of the day. Dinner was awkward, as they had guests for the first time since Gaylord's "illness," and they were curious as to just what fever and disease he had had.

Mara retired early to her room and hoped that Gaylord would retire also, as he had seemed weary and distracted during dinner. It had been difficult for him, his first dinner engagement since his wounding.

She was in bed when she heard him calling her. "Mara, Mara, come here!"

It was the fretful imperious call she had heard often during his illness. She rose at once, flung on her negligee, and went to his bedroom. It was lit dimly with a few candles near the bedside.

"What is it? Are you feverish, Gaylord?" She went over to his bedside anxiously and touched his forehead. He did seem warm and weary.

"I want to talk to you!" he said angrily. "I want to ask you some questions!"

She sighed. She sat down at his good side and stroked her palm gently over his face. That always seemed to soothe him. "But you are tired, and so am I, señor," she said mildly. "Cannot it wait until another time? You have had a heavy day, with all the guests—"

"Then come to bed with me," he demanded.

She hesitated, then slipped under the covers, after removing her negligee. She thought to lie quietly at his side and put her head on his shoulder. But he moved to bend over her and study her face with fever-bright eyes. At least, she thought it might be fever, until he bent and began to kiss her mouth with hard strength, anger, passion mingled.

She trembled a little at the passion of his mouth, opened against her soft lips. She wanted to respond, she wanted to hold him in her arms and reply to him and feed her starved love on the caresses he used to punish her.

Why not? Why not? she thought. It would only be for one night; he would soon tire of her and go to sleep. He would tire of her one day and leave her. Why not have a memory to hold to herself when he was gone?

Timidly, unsure of herself, she put her arms about his neck. He bent more closely to her, and his bruising kisses turned gentle on her opening lips. They kissed, long, more deeply, and his hand began to caress her shoulder.

"Mara, Mara, Mara," he whispered demandingly into her ear, as he kissed the ear lobe, and below it down to her neck. He buried his face against her pulsing throat, and she surrendered entirely.

In the silent room she could only hear her own hurried breathing, and his, as they made love to each other, mouths pressing more deeply, hands caressing fervently, bodies pressing more tightly, until—they were one. And he was gentle at last, holding her, bringing her with him to the heights of ecstasy.

CHAPTER 13

As Gaylord regained his strength, their relationship seemed to have changed. He demanded her attentions as his right. He would come into her bedroom casually at any hour of the day or night and sit beside her, tease her, talk to her lightly or seriously.

He told her a little about his mission to Spain, cautiously, warning her not to discuss it with anyone, not even José. "For I know you have complete confidence in him, but I trust very few persons! If I can discover the way that the people wish to be governed, and my government can aid in turning them to a right path, I shall have my reward. But discretion is of the utmost necessity, you can see that, Mara."

"Yes, I understand, Gaylord. But I—I do not see—" She paused and studied him with troubled eyes. He did not seem to trust her in some matters, yet in others he was being rather reckless in his confidence.

"You do not see what?" he demanded. "Come over here, Mara, you are too far away!" They were in his study; she was sitting across the desk from him.

Automatically she stood up and came around the desk to him, before she realized how quick had been her response to his every order. He smiled as he drew her down on his knee and put his arms about her. His head went down on her shoulder, he nuzzled against her soft throat, where the muslin frills fell away.

"Ah, I can see I am going to have a good obedient wife," he murmured mischievously. "I am training you well, eh? I like this little bit here," and he kissed the soft flesh beneath her ear. She flushed and turned away, stiffening. His arms tightened. "No, don't pull away! You are doing quite well! Just relax and say, 'Si, señor, yes, sir, I will do whatever you please!' Say it, Mara!"

"No, I will not!" she cried out rebelliously against his teasing. She tried to pull away, but he laughed and pulled her more tightly to him. She felt the hardness of his thighs against the softness of her hips. His warmth warmed her cool body, his lips were teasing at her even as his words teased her mind.

"Oh, you will one day, I shall have you trained to my hand!" he told her. She glared up into his face bravely. But his eyes were not laughing, they were blazing blue and direct. "Ah, you are an independent one! But you see, Mara, you do not have to be independent any longer. You have a husband to decide for you, and protect you, and forbid you to get into any danger! Sometimes when I think how you rode in boys' clothing in the night, and fought duels with your sword, I think I am mad! No, I think you were mad! Did you not realize you might be killed?"

Her eyes opened wide. "But of course I understood that," she told him, puzzled. "Everyone ran the risk. We were prepared for it. I carried no identification. I had thought to cut my hair short like a boy's, but Juana screamed when I suggested—"

"Your hair! You would have cut it!" His big hand thrust up through the soft waves. "Absolutely not! I should forbid it also. Your glorious hair! It was bad enough that you should run into danger—"

She sighed impatiently. "You do not understand! It was necessary! And José had trained me carefully! And besides—why, señor, you were in the same work! You spied! You told me so. Only your fast horses got you away! There. You were in the same danger as I. What is the difference?"

"I am a man. You are a woman," he said decidedly, his palm warm against the back of her neck. "That is the difference, and all the difference. Do not pout! Have I not been teaching you the difference between a man and a woman?"

Now he was laughing at her again, and she flushed red as a rose at the laughing meaning in his eyes. He leaned over and pressed his open lips to hers as she began to protest again. His kisses turned her weak and dazed. She was answering them before she knew.

She did not know why she yielded so quickly to him. There was a betrayal in her soft body, a desire to know his desire, a hunger that would not be satisfied except temporarily when he held her and caressed her. She longed to hear words of love from him, but thought she never would. She wanted to say "I love you" to him and have him respond with warmth. But that could never be.

She must be satisfied with this, she thought, as she leaned back against him and felt his hands roaming her soft slimness, strained her to him, his lips on her throat, on her arms. Yes, there was passion in him for her—but nothing else. And when he tired of her—

The butler knocked discreetly on the door several times. Gaylord finally raised his head and sighed, "Always interruptions! Thank God we can be alone at night! All right, Mara, jump down. I shall continue our—discussion—at a later time!"

He laughed again at her vivid blush. She took the opportunity to escape when the butler came in with his message. She went to the drawing room where Enid was welcoming the first of the afternoon guests, pausing only to smooth her hair in front of the hall mirror. She could do nothing about the rosiness of her cheeks, the starriness of her blue eyes.

Enid asked her to pour tea, and she was thankful for the small task to get her mind off her thoughts. Little Jennie came around to take the cakes to the guests, and Fergus trotted about until he was satisfied with his cakes in the corner. Jennie settled down beside Mara and listened intently to the conversation Mara was having in Spanish with a diffident lady of the diplomatic corps.

Enid sent her a grateful speaking glance. She had trouble with Spanish—except when she was with her lover, Ramón, thought Mara drily. The language of love had been much easier for Enid to learn than the language of diplomacy.

She chatted with the lady, easily, with half her mind. The lady wished to discuss fashions, a ball to be held, the latest gossip about a French lady who had returned hastily to Paris following her discovery with a Spaniard of dubious reputation. Mara could follow it with no difficulty and still think about Gaylord.

Enid came over to her presently. "Where is that husband of yours, Mara?" she whispered. "The men are arriving, and one of them is most desirous of conversing with him. Do fetch him away from his work!"

Mara hesitated, then shrugged. Gaylord would come or not, as he himself chose. She could only take him the message. She slipped away from the company and went back to the hallway.

The door to Gaylord's study was open about three inches. She heard his voice, speaking gravely, clearly. She hesitated, frowning. She did not want to interrupt him if he were discussing something serious with a diplomat.

Then she heard the light clear tones of the other party. Vivienne Desmond. There was no mistaking her lazy sensuous drawl. "But Gaylord —it doesn't need to make any difference between us!" she was saying.

Mara froze. Her hand was on the door; she withdrew it as though it were burned. She turned to leave, but hesitated again. She wanted to know, her tormented soul longed to know for certain, to know he was unworthy of love, that she had no chance to win his sure love.

"You always came back to me between your affairs," said the light assured tone. "Did I reproach you? Do I reproach you now? No, she is a silly little chit, with no breeding, no manners. She cannot interest you for long! Oh, I know you so well, Gaylord, darling! I know your motives for marrying her! You have never changed! I read you like a book!"

"Do you, Vivienne? I suppose you do," he said

with a grave voice. "Yes, we have known each other quite well. You return to England soon, do you?"

"Yes, I must. But I want you to promise me, you will follow shortly, darling! Our affair can continue as though nothing had interrupted it! In England it will be easy to rid yourself of your little burden. She is rather a pretty thing, now that you have dressed her properly! You can find her someone of her own age, someone suitable, and wash your hands of the whole mess. Her father should have known better than to appoint you guardian!"

She laughed, a light tinkle of amusement. Gaylord did not join her. Mara, standing rigidly, trembling a little, listened for his reply.

It came, cold, clear. "Yes, I think the whole matter was a mistake. However, it has turned out well, I am thankful for that. In England, everything can be settled as best for all of us. Meantime, I trust to your discretion—"

Mara waited for no more. She turned and ran up the stairs, straight as an arrow to her bedroom. Shaking, she entered and found herself alone. Juana was probably gossiping in the kitchen with her favorite confidante, the parlormaid. Mara locked her door and went to sit in a chair near the window. She was cold, so cold that she trembled, and her hands clasped each other desperately.

So it was true, what she had guessed and suspected. Gaylord was a flirt like her father. He had married Mara to get his hands on her fortune. When he tired of her, when he had her fortune securely in his hands, he would desert her.

And she had been stupid enough to fall in love with him! She raised her hands to her face, pressed them slowly to her eyes. She could not cry, she felt too deeply wounded for tears. It went to her soul like a hot knife, cleaving through tender flesh. The pain would come later. Now she was incredulous, gasping, holding her breath.

Gaylord, Gaylord. So tender to her, his kisses pressing so sweetly to her flesh. Now the knife in her back. The knife—deeper than a sword. He was carrying on his affair with Vivienne Desmond, he had as much as admitted it. He would get rid of Mara and marry her off to someone of his choosing, someone young, someone he could control. And he would keep on controlling Mara, through her pliable husband!

Oh, no, she thought. My lord husband, you control me no longer! I will not accept it again!

She would pull him out of her heart and out of her soul, with both fierce, ruthless hands! She would not endure that he should reside there, her loved one, her lover, the man who had gotten past her fierce defenses and into her heart. She would not be tormented so! She would not continue to love such a one as he had proved to be!

Suddenly she was remembering, remembering her mother's last days. They had been in the apartment in London. Her mother had grown weaker, lying finally on the chaise longue, with a robe over her, her little thin hands fluttering like white butterflies in the early winter dusk.

"Shall I write to father, shall I ask him to come, because you are ill?" Mara had asked over and over, anxiously. "Please, mother, maybe he can find a doctor to make you well."

"No, no, my child. I do not wish to become well," her mother had said finally, bitterly, turning her face away. She seemed to struggle with herself. "When he left me—I died. Ah, my child, you do not understand that. But when my darling left me, when he said he was weary of me, that I was too simple, too—ah, it hurts yet. God, it hurts yet." And she had pressed her small hand to the narrow breast as though it pained her to breathe.

Then her mother had grown worse. The doctor had come, had shaken his head, had whispered to her nurse, who pulled a long face. Her mother had watched them, quietly, not in a panic, not in fear, but as though they said something that she welcomed.

That night she called to the child, who slept now in the same room, on a narrow couch near the bed of the dying woman.

"Mara, Mara?"

Mara had wakened, rubbed her eyes, jumped up, run to her mother, to find her panting for breath, half-sitting up.

"Mara, my darling, write to your father. Beg him to come," she breathed, gasping. "Listen—I want to see—his face—once more! Beg him—if he will come to me—I will ask for no more than an hour—beg him—beg—"

"I will, mother, I will—oh, mother—" For her mother had fallen back against the pillows, a vague smile on her lips.

"His—picture! Then—his picture. I cannot—wait—for him—" her mother had whispered.

Mara snatched the small miniature from the table and held it in her hand so her mother could see it.

"Ah—Brandon—it is Anne—begging—Brandon—" her mother muttered, and her head fell back. Even before Mara had laid down the picture and leaned to her, the child had known with some sure fatalistic instinct. Her mother was dead.

And now it was to happen to her. Mara stared with dry burning eyes at the glory of the sunlight in the gardens below. It was to be her fate—to love someone who did not love her, who would soon tire of her, discard her, yet hold to her with strength of iron. He would control her life, jerk her like a puppet—from a distance.

She would know no more the sure strength of his arms in bed, the teasing laughing voice as he

demanded response to his kisses. She would not
know again the touch of his mouth on her throat,
the slow rising passion and heat of him as he
taught her what it was to know a man's desire.
Her body would not waken and thrill with strange
ecstasy.

She would be empty—alone—unless he made
her marry some young man he could control. She
winced with pain then, closing her eyes with a
shudder. How could she bear it for any other man
in the world to touch her? No, she could not endure that; she could not bear it to marry someone
else.

If only she could be alone. Alone in the dark
house where she had lived in Madrid. Live in the
shadows, creep about like a wounded animal,
until the pain diminished, and she could work
again. She could bury herself in her work, she
thought. She could read and write and walk in
the dark gardens, under the trees, and rest—rest
—until death—

To go from this house of light, La Casa Dorada, the house of gold and sunshine, to the darkness of her former home, would be like going
from life to death. But there was no help for it,
she would have to go.

"If only—I had not known him—" she muttered. She despised herself for falling in love with
someone just like her father. She had had warning

enough. Her father in his loose behavior was the example she had had.

She knew how men were, the charming loose men whose eyes roved from one pretty woman to a more beautiful one. Who took a mistress and discarded her. Who took a wife and left her, and left the child.

She pressed her hands to her breasts. At least her mother had had a child. She had said often that Mara was her only comfort, and she had held Mara's face in her thin white hands and studied lovingly the dark hair and vivid blue eyes, declaring she was the image of her father "with more kindness in you, Mara, darling."

If Mara had had a child—a son?

But she had not. She would not. She would live in the dark house in Madrid—live and die alone. It was her punishment for having been so foolish as to love someone like Gaylord Humphrey. And then a quick vision came of him, of his laughing teasing mouth, the brilliant blue eyes, the demanding light in his face as he pulled her closer to him.

And the pain started.

CHAPTER 14

Juana knocked at the door and called to her. Mara finally aroused herself from her daze and grief and went to unlock the door and let her in.

The maid looked at her in a long worried gaze. "My little dove, they are calling for you from the drawing room. What shall I tell them? Are you ill? Your face is so flushed, your hands are shaking." She took the small white hands in her large brown ones and chafed them lovingly, murmuring to her charge.

Mara could scarcely speak. She was impatient at the interruption of her thoughts. She had plans to make, she must leave, she must get away.

She shook her head as Juana pleaded with her. "No, I am not well. No, I cannot go down. Tell them—tell them I cannot come down."

But even as she was saying it, her husband came in the door. One look at his angry face and blazing blue eyes, and she knew she was in for some trouble. "Mara, why have you not come down? You were there earlier, the guests know you are not ill! Come at once!"

Juana left the room hastily, with the air of one escaping wrath with great relief. She closed the hall door after her.

Mara faced her husband, her chin up, ready to do battle. The conversation she had overheard was stinging her to the soul. She looked at him and thought of how corrupt and bad he was, how he had charmed her, how he had mercilessly taken her life into his two large brown hands and molded it the way he wished.

"I do not wish to be ordered about by you, my lord," she said very coldly, very disdainfully. "I will not come. I have other matters to do!"

He stared at her as though she had run mad. He seemed to catch his breath at her defiance. "You—what? You will do as I say!"

"No, I think not!"

Her chin up, she gazed steadily at him. If he had touched her, she would have struck out at him like a wounded animal. But he stood his distance, his legs apart, as though prepared to fight a duel.

"Mara, listen to me. It is necessary for us to return to England in the near future. Meantime, there is much good we can do for the Spaniards. You know my mission. If you will talk to your friends, they trust you—"

"Your mission is—your mission, my lord!" she

said brutally. "I have no part in it. You may complete your mission and return to England as soon as you choose! As for me, I shall remain here. Madrid is my home. I shall return to my own home and live there!"

Her blue eyes blazed into his surprised blue gaze. "You? In your home—This is your home! Where I live is your home!"

She thought of the words he had exchanged with Mrs. Desmond, and her heart hardened to a lump of ice. "No, señor, it is not! Our farce of a marriage is at an end! I shall end it, here and now! We care—nothing for each other. You may return to England today, if you wish! What you do has nothing to do with me!"

"How dare you speak like that?" His breath came in a hissing fury. He strode over to her and caught at her slim arms with his large hands. His fingers gripped so tightly that she thought there would be bruises on them the next day. She did not move, defying him with her steady look, her half-shut eyes. "You—are—my—wife! You will go with me! You shall live in England and learn a wife's true place! You will learn to obey me! Mara, how dare you say such things! How can you?"

A wife's true place! She listened to him with such intense bitterness that he must have felt it. She was thinking of how it would be in England, with Mara meekly doing her husband's will, waiting for him to come to her bed at night—if he so

chose! Or waiting in the background if he chose
to take Mrs. Desmond out to a ball, go to her
home, live with her, sleep with her, show her the
passion and desire he felt for her—

Oh, no, oh no, no, no! thought Mara. She would
not be callously handled, mistreated, abandoned
as her mother had been! She was too proud for
that!

She cut in on his blast of words, as he was saying, "You shall obey me! When we return to England in a couple of weeks, you shall come with
me, with no protest! I know you are fond of Madrid, but we can return here, sometime in the future, for visits. I do not mean for you to forget
your friends entirely. José shall be provided for,
there are other British families who need a good
tutor, and I shall see him well-placed before I
leave—"

"Thank you, señor! You would sell him also?
He would not thank you! He is quite a capable
person, and well-respected! He does not ask your
favors, nor do I ask for him!" she raged.

"What do you mean—sell him also? What are
you talking about?" His sharp eyes stared down
at her. His fingers bit cruelly into her upper arms.

She bit her tongue. That had slipped out. She
had been thinking of how he planned to arrange
her marriage to some pliant young man. She said,
more quietly, "I mean—José can manage his own
affairs. He will be in demand as a tutor, I am

sure. Please allow him to make his own arrangements when you leave. As for me, I plan to make my own arrangements, also. I shall live here, quietly, and continue my studies, as I told you before."

"You shall not! You are my wife! You belong to me," and his voice was raging angry, a sharp contrast to her soft tones. "Why would you even consider staying? What holds you here?"

She stared up at him. What held her here in Madrid? She had lived here for years, but living apart from him, having known him, would be like exile from paradise. Bitter though it had been, the few weeks of their marriage had become the peak of her life. She had known ecstasy, caresses, a man's passion—and her own growing irrepressible love for him. Nothing in this world would ever again matter as much to her as the touch of his hand, the sight of his face, the blaze in his eyes, the tenderness of his arms.

She remembered again her mother's anguished cry to behold her husband's face once more, and she closed her eyes in terror. Such pain should not have to be endured.

"What is it? What is it, Mara? I demand to know! Your face—you are in pain! I know you!— what makes you feel this way?" he commanded imperiously, his touch gentling. "Do you feel thus to be leaving Madrid? I shall make life as easy for you in England as possible! You shall have whatever you wish, live in London, or in the country when you will. There shall be books, your studies. There are tutors there to teach you what you wish. You need not be ever in society if you do not care for it! I promise you—I shall not be a tyrant, Mara."

Was his tone pleading? It could not be. He was trying his charm on her once more.

"I know the gardens here are beautiful, but you shall have English gardens, with roses and honeysuckle. The house is old; it has not been refurnished since I inherited it. It shall be redecorated as you wish, in any colors you choose, with the furnishings you like. Only tell me what you want, Mara! Why do you not speak?"

She must not be fooled by him once more! She warned herself, against the tide of weakness that wanted to wash over her. What woman in love could resist the passionate wooing of his voice? the gentleness and anxiety of his tone? his words, so thoughtful, so—so deceptive? She knew why he wanted her pleased and quiet.

It was so he might go off to be with Mrs. Desmond as he chose!

"You close your eyes and your heart against me, Mara! I will not have it!" Anger was growing in his voice as she remained stubbornly silent and resistant to him. His clasp tightened more cruelly again. "Listen to me, tell me what you want! Tell me, and I will do it—"

She opened her eyes, gazed up at his chin. She could no longer look into his eyes; she would betray herself.

"I wish to be alone," she said with deadly quiet. "I wish to remain—alone—in Madrid, in my *own house*. I would return to *my house* and live there. Alone. I would not belong to any—any man! I will live my own life, as I choose! I will not be any man's puppet!"

His eyes blazed down at hers. "You—you do not know what you ask!" he roared, furious once more. "I know now! You love that—that puppy! That Ramón Olivera! That guardsman, with his uniform and his handsome young looks. That is it! He is Spanish, and you must love him for it! Oh, no, Mara, I shall not let you stay in Madrid to be near your lover! I will not endure that!"

She opened her lips to say Ramón was not her lover, to deny that indignantly. But she kept silent. Let him think what he chose. He might let her stay, might divorce her, might free her.

Her husband shook her in exasperation. Her fine blue-black hair flew about her face. "Oh, you infuriate me," he said finally, when she would not speak. "Very well, be silent then! Keep to your room until you are in a better mood! But I shall make you pay dearly for your defiance of me! And do not think I will allow you to remain in Madrid. When we remove to England, you shall go with us!"

And he stormed from the room and slammed the door after him. Mara shuddered and put her hands to her numb arms. He had hurt her with his fingers, but her heart was more bruised. She could not, would not stay here. She must leave him. She must—or be humiliated and humbled. She could not live with herself if she so betrayed her own ideals.

She would not remain with a man who could be like this, so domineering, so demanding of her morals—while so lax with his own! It was not fair, it was not right. She would not stay. She would leave, hide herself away, until he became tired of her "whims" and "moods." Then he would let her alone.

CHAPTER 15

Mara wasted no time. Anger drove her on. Swiftly she changed to her riding habit. Juana stayed away, no doubt thinking she and Gaylord were having a "fine quarrel."

She gathered up several objects she wished to take with her. She took one pistol of her brace, some shot for it, and after a hesitation her own special long slim light sword with the shining deadly blade.

She wrapped the pistol and sword in an older gown, added a boy's shirt and trousers, boots, the picture of her mother. She gathered them all into a loose bundle—then whirled around.

She had had the sensation of being watched —and she was. Jennie and Fergus stood at the doorway of her room, watching silently, with the wide-eyed curiosity of their age.

"Where are you going, Auntie Mara?" asked Fergus gravely.

"And with your sword, Auntie Mara?" added

Jennie eagerly. "Is your enemy around? There is a man who watched the villa yesterday and the day before; José saw him. Are they after you now?"

"No, no," said Mara impatiently, flushing. "I— I am just going home, children. Only you must not tell anyone where I have gone!"

Jennie whispered breathlessly, spots of color on her pink and white cheeks. "Oh, I know it is more than that, Auntie Mara! You are going to have an adventure! Oh, may I go also?"

"Of course not!" she said, more sharply than she had intended. "I am simply going home. But no one is to know this!"

"Uncle Gaylord says your home is with him," piped up Fergus.

Mara flushed vividly and turned from them. "No—no, it is not," she said in a low tone, and drew a deep sigh. If only that were really true. "Goodbye—Jennifer—Fergus—" She bent and kissed them and then went down the hall, aware they were watching her.

She sped down the back hall to the kitchens. The maids looked up curiously as she went past. She dropped her cloth bundle in the back hall and went out to speak to a groom. He soon had her mare saddled and brought round to her.

She swung into the saddle with the feeling of escaping. She held the bundle before her and started out cautiously at a walk down the gravel path, as though to ride in the woods as she often did.

It was late afternoon. The sun was sinking; the world was growing dusky with shadows. She rode, taking to the side roads she knew so well by now. Then down into the heart of the city, keeping the mare to the grassy side. This was her mare; Gaylord had given her to his wife. It was all she would keep of their brief marriage. She had left her rings, her bracelets, all the jewelry he had given her, including the wedding ring.

He would soon discard her. No man wanted such an unwilling obstinate wife, she thought.

It was quite dark when she reached her old home. She looked at the dark windows and doors and sighed. She had forgotten how very gloomy and dark it was. After La Casa Dorada, the house of gold, the house of sunlight and laughter, it looked the more dark and depressing.

She rode around to the stables, slid off the mare and unsaddled her. She wiped her down and saw her settled with food and water before she went to a side door. She unlocked the door and went inside.

Her footsteps echoed eerily through the house of shadows. She hesitated as she reached the hallway. It was cold here. She would freeze—no, there were blankets in the bedrooms upstairs. She would go to her old suite of- rooms and make it comfortable. If wood was there, she could build a fire.

She had locked the door after herself. She was used to being alone, at least she had been in the old days. Now, the house seemed so desolate, so empty. No servants there, no Juana, no José. Just Mara, alone, bruised, aching, with a need to hide herself.

Quietly she ascended the stairs up to her old rooms. She opened the door and sniffed at the musty odor. She should have come over before this, to see how the house was doing. She set her bundle on a sofa, opened it, then went to look for blankets. The cupboards were amply filled, and she drew out several blankets thankfully. She would not freeze tonight.

Tomorrow she must recall one of the maids and a cook. They would shop for her; she would obtain money from the vault in her father's study —unless Gaylord had removed it all. She frowned. Money might be a problem.

Food—blankets—heat.

She found wood in the bedroom, piled beside the fireplace. From experience she knew it would take quite a pile to get those vast rooms warm. She set the fire, started it, and was rewarded by a warm crackling and some light. She made the bed with fresh sheets and the blankets and thought she would do very well.

She settled down in a huge chair in front of the fire, wrapped in one of the blankets. She had set out her sword and her pistol, though she had thought she would not have need of them. Still— she was alone in the vast house. Sometimes vagrants got in.

Inevitably her thoughts went back to La Casa Dorada and to Gaylord. He would have discovered her departure by this time, and she sighed as she thought how he would rage. But he would hardly come after her. He would not so humiliate himself. He must accept the fact that she had left him and planned to remain away. Besides, this would make it easier for him to divorce her.

She toyed with the thought of his coming for her, of his possessive anger, of his demands that she remain his wife. Would he come? No, she thought not.

She was sitting curled before the fire, lost in her bitter thoughts of Gaylord and Vivienne Desmond, when she heard a sound.

A door opening? Something moving? A clatter? She frowned, her senses suddenly alert.

She started up, as she heard a voice that echoed through the hall.

"Mara! Mara Pearsall! Oh, the grand señora, the lady!" the voice yelled in Spanish.

She tensed, suddenly frightened, on guard.

The voice came again, taunting. "I know you are here! I knew you would return to your cave!

Come out, traitor! Come out, and see your fate!"

It was Lope Sanchez-Garcia. He must have followed her.

Swiftly she remembered what Jennie had said, that José had thought someone was watching the house. Enough Spaniards of the enemy side had visited La Casa Dorada to guess easily at the state of affairs between Mara and her husband. So Lope Sanchez-Garcia had guessed that Mara would run away, would leave him!

The fire in the fireplace—he would smell the smoke and come up here!

Mara snatched up her sword, the pistol and balls, and a blanket. She ran out of the suite of rooms and headed for the back hallway. Already boots were thumping up the front steps. Sanchez-Garcia and his men made no secret of their presence. They feared nothing from her.

"The wench has been run to ground," Sanchez-Garcia yelled as he came up the stairs. "She will be dead before long. Say your prayers, Señora! I will allow you as much time as you allowed Cristobal!"

Mara was running lightly up the back stairs to the third floor. It was pitch black up there, no windows open, but she knew it like the back of her hand. She ran for a room that was sanctuary, the schoolroom, with its immense closets, the other rooms opening from it. She could hide from room to room.

Lope Sanchez-Garcia had reached her rooms. He yelled in triumph, calling to her as he went in. She could hear the roar of his voice as she hid herself in the schoolroom, behind the darkened drapes. She loaded her pistol with cold but steady hands. She had one shot—and she hoped it would be for him. Then she had her sword for the others. She wondered how many of them there would be, if she could frighten them off.

Her best bet was to hide. They might tire of searching the house.

She stood in silence, as she heard the men tramping from room to room, calling out to her, yelling insults they hoped she would answer. She began to turn colder, there in the cold rooms, after the warmth of the fireplace.

They came up the stairs finally, to the third floor. Sanchez-Garcia growled out his orders. "Spread out and search from room to room. You —guard the front stairs, you the back. She must not be allowed to escape me this time!"

From the tramping of feet she guessed there must be at least four men with him. She bit her lips, her eyes wide against the darkness. How many could she kill? Would they succeed in killing her? The next hours would tell.

The flare of a torch lit the schoolroom, and she had to fight herself to keep from screaming. A man walked in, his shadow taller than himself as he walked about searching. She stood still behind the drapes, scarcely daring to breathe.

Then a man called from the front stairs, called in Spanish, "Master, some men are coming! They are unlocking the front doors!"

Sanchez-Garcia growled a curse. "Who are they?"

"The British lord," came the answer.

Mara's breath caught in a gasp; she could scarcely control herself now. Not Gaylord, he would not come—he would not—

"Mara!" came his familiar imperative tone. "Mara, where are you? Come here at once!"

The utter silence of the men waiting told her their plans. They would kill him as he came up the stairs.

She held her breath. They were so close to her —but she must warn Gaylord—

She waited—then she screamed loudly, shrilly. "Gaylord! Beware! Beware! Beware! The enemies are here!"

She heard Lope Sanchez-Garcia cursing her roundly. "Find her! She is screaming—"

"I hear her—she is in this room!" cried a man, very close to her. He snatched aside the drapes; she fired her pistol directly at him, and he dropped.

The man was dead; he had dropped with only a groan. She stepped away from the drapes and held her slim sword ready.

She watched the doorway. A torch came closer,

then a man entered, sidling around the door, one of Sanchez-Garcia's men. She waited, and he was staring at her, his eyes round and flaring in the torchlight.

Then Sanchez-Garcia came in, his sword at the ready. He saw her, and he began to grin.

"So—the bitch is run to ground," he said triumphantly, and came at her swiftly, his face dark with the fury of mad anger. His sword was long, but so was hers. She held it ready, side-stepped agilely, and his sword went past her shoulder.

He recovered, stepped back and parried her thrust neatly. The shock of it went down her arm, almost numbing it. He was fighting with the insanity of a madman. She saw his eyes blazing black pools of hate as he fought her.

She saved her breath. He was cursing her. "I have waited long to find and kill you! Now, no one shall defeat me! You she-devil, damn you, damn—"

He thrust forward, she parried it, letting the blade slide harmlessly from her hilt. Instantly she thrust at him, and the tip of her sword caught at his shoulder, ripping the fabric; she recovered and sprang back, ready for the next thrust.

There were cries in the hallway, the ring of steel crashing on steel, a pistol's blast. Then Gaylord appeared in the doorway. She saw him from the corner of her eye; she dared not look away from the set hard face of her enemy.

He thrust again, lunged closer, and forced her back against the drapes. Her foot caught on the outflung arm of the dead man. She stumbled, went to her knees. Lope Sanchez-Garcia was after her in the instant.

But behind him was Gaylord, his long sword ready. He tapped Sanchez-Garcia on the shoulder. "Turn this way—I am here," said the Britisher in a cool deadly drawl.

Sanchez-Garcia flung about; his fury had betrayed his life. The two men fought, this time more evenly matched. Mara, fighting for breath, leaned against the wall and watched, her light slim sword up and ready if her husband needed her aid.

José appeared in the doorway, then Ramón Olivera, both with bloody swords. They watched, and she knew from the way they watched the duel that the other men were dispatched. Their entire attention was on the fight to the death before them.

Sanchez-Garcia was heavier than Gaylord, his sword held in tiring hands. His face was ghastly now, dripping with sweat, his black eyes betraying fear. It was always so with him, thought Mara, when the odds were not heavily in his favor. She watched, eyes narrowed, breath held, as they fought.

He seemed to remember how Gaylord had been flung off balance before. He began to curse, panting. "Your wife—damn her—you and her lover come to her rescue, eh? Damn her. Damn her soul to hell! She will betray you—as she betrays all men—and her father before her all women! She is no good, as you have found, eh? No good, no good—"

Gaylord lunged forward, and his sword went into the guard, past the long sword of his enemy. It went in cleanly, into the chest, so that the older man seemed to hang on it, helplessly, clutching at the hilt as Gaylord drove it furiously inside. No blood spurted; the sword held it all.

The man fell slowly, his face passing from surprise to blankness. When he was down, Gaylord withdrew his sword slowly, and now the blood spurted briefly, then stopped.

José went over to him, bent down, looked into the eyes, felt the hand. "He is dead," he said without expression.

"So die all such," blurted out Ramón Olivera. "What a devil he is! To chase after a defenseless woman."

Now Gaylord looked at Mara, at the sword held ready in her hand, at the dead man at her feet. "Not—quite—defenseless, Olivera," he said quietly, with a gleam of pride in his tone. "This is a fighter, eh? What a woman!" He stepped back, wiped the sword deliberately on the dead man's coat, then wiped his own hands on his handkerchief.

José went over to Mara, who was beginning to tremble with reaction. "Come, Mara, we take you home now," he said.

"This is my home," she said, her chin up, bleak pride in her tone. "I stay here!"

"God, woman, no wonder your husband loses patience with you," said José, with the beginnings of a smile. "Come, you must return home with us. We cannot rescue you every night! I need my dinner and my rest!"

Her husband had scarcely glanced at her since the look at her sword. He seemed engaged in studying the bodies of the two dead men.

Mara hesitated. She did not want to remain in the house with the dead men. And knowing law and the police as she did, she thought it might be tomorrow before the bodies were removed. And reports must be made and signed before lawyers, and all that.

"Well—I suppose I must go—back," she said flatly.

José escorted her past her husband and Ramón and down the stairs. She paused at her room to gather up her bundle, and José put out the fire in her fireplace. It was José who escorted her down to the carriage. Her husband was so silent, she kept looking at him uneasily. They put her in the carriage. Ramón offered to ride the mare back, but they thought she could wait until morning.

She did ask one question. "How did—you know

—that I was here?" She forced the question past a tight throat.

"The children went to José; he brought them to me. When we learned you were going back—home—with your sword and pistol, we feared. Then José told me that you had been watched and followed for days. We came at once."

"I told the children—not to tell," she said, in a sort of wailing protest.

"Fortunately, they had more sense than to listen to you," said her husband drily. He glanced at her to see if he had roused her temper. She turned her face away and stared out the window of the carriage.

They took her back to La Casa Dorada in silence.

CHAPTER 16

The house was ablaze with lights as the carriage rolled up to the doorway. The butler ran down the steps to the carriage door and faltered in Spanish, "My lady, you are safe! Praise God, may his name be thanked, you are safe!"

She thanked him, rather surprised at his emotion. She had thought some of the servants liked her, but his expressed concern did please her.

She accepted his hand to help her out of the carriage. Gaylord did not come near her, but waited behind her as she went slowly inside.

His voice spoke harshly. "Go into the drawing room. You also, José, you Olivera. There are matters we must discuss."

Mara did not protest. She was too keyed up to sleep. Lyman Chandler and Enid came from the drawing room. Jennie and Fergus bounded after them excitedly, piping up when they saw Mara.

They all returned to the huge room. Mara sank down on the sofa, shaking now, and cold. Ramón stood guard at the door, his face uneasy. José stood near him, his round face expressionless, his brown eyes narrowed and keen, waiting.

Gaylord turned to his brother-in-law. "We found her at the house," he said, as though weary, his face intensely strained. "Lope Sanchez-Garcia was there. He and four of his men lie dead in the house. I killed him."

Lyman stared at him. "My God," he said blankly. "Uh—was it necessary? Oh, yes, God, a foolish question." He pressed his hand to his forehead. "The embassy must be notified. The bodies—questions—we will get the lawyers—"

"In the morning. It will wait." Gaylord stared down at the sword he still held in his hand, then carefully laid it on the mantel. Jennie and Fergus stared up at it, their mouths open in fascination, their eyes bright with awe as their childish imaginations worked on what they had been told.

Enid was sitting beside Mara. She reached over and took one of her cold hands in hers. "You poor child. Why did you run off like that?" she reproached. "Just because you quarreled with Gaylord—the danger of it! I'll be glad to get you back to England—"

"She is not returning with me," said Gaylord flatly. He turned his back to the mantel and stood with legs apart, as though braced for their amazement. "I have decided—she does not wish to return. She may stay here—if she so chooses."

There was a heavy silence. Mara's lips moved, but she could not speak. Leave her here? To die? He was going to do that? But it was what she had said, what she had proclaimed she wanted.

His gaze was closely on her face, as though he would read her as soon as she thought. She gazed up at him.

"Yes, Mara," he said quietly. "If you wish to marry Ramón, if you feel so strongly about it that you would run into danger so recklessly, I will—release you. I will obtain a divorce and let you marry. I cannot—continue—to hold you—against your will—" Sweat stood out on his forehead as he said the words.

"Ramón?" she whispered. "But I—I—" Enid had dropped her hand, and Mara saw the white hands clasped tightly, nervously together. She thought, but I cannot betray her! And let him think so, it is less humiliating than to know that Mara loved her husband too desperately to endure his affair with Vivienne Desmond.

"But Auntie Mara does not love Ramón!" Jennie blurted out excitedly. "It is Mama! She meets him in the gardens! She kisses him!"

Mara gasped, but it was drowned out by Fergus, bubbling out the secrets like a juicy orange spurts its juices. "It is Mama," he echoed, his eyes wide and wondering. "She tells us it is too cold to play in the garden. Then she goes out and meets Ramón there. And we aren't allowed to come!"

There was a dazed incredulous silence in the room. Then Ramón Olivera took a step forward. His handsome dark Spanish face was drawn. "It is my fault, entirely my fault. I—I loved her—I could not stay away. It is entirely my fault—"

"No, no, Ramón!" Enid burst out, then began to cry. She sobbed into her hands. "It is my fault —I was so silly—but I had never—and he was so kind—and Lyman was so busy—I am sorry—Mara was blamed, but I could not tell—oh, God, I am sorry!"

Mara touched her head gently, stroked the blond hair. Lyman Chandler stood as though hit by a heavy blow, staring down at his wife incredulously. The children retreated from the scene, holding hands, backing up cautiously to the windows, now they had told the dread secret that had been burgeoning inside their small selves.

Jennie did offer one final secret, breathlessly, "And Auntie Mara has a sword, and she did kill some men, and José knows about it, and they did fight—"

"That will do, Jennie," said Gaylord, seeming to wake from a daze. He came over to Mara slowly, then so swiftly that she winced, he dropped to his knees before her. He took her hands in his, grabbing them, holding them hard. His face was twisted. "Then, why, why, Mara? Why were you leaving me?" he cried.

Mara was too tired and dazed to be diplomatic or careful. She blurted out the truth, even as the children had. "Because you do not love me. Because you love Vivienne Desmond. I overheard you speaking to her. You said you would carry on the affair!"

"I—said—" he stared at her, his face very close to hers. He was too close, she tried to back from him, but his body was pressed to her knees, his hands gripped hers ruthlessly. "I never said—"

"She had told me—that you—always returned to her—between affairs. She said that, I knew it was the truth. And you—I overheard you today —you will meet her in England!" she cried, outraged. "You will divorce me—and marry me to someone you can control—and continue with— her—with her!"

"Oh, Mara," he breathed, and his face began to glow with understanding, and a fire she could not understand. "Oh, I am punished. Oh, God, I thought only to devil her, I never dreamed you would—oh, my God!"

She fought to pull her hands from his, but he held them all the more tightly. "Let me go!" she stormed at him. "I will not stay with you! I will not endure—"

"No, Mara, I will never let you go now! You love no one else; I will see to it that you come to love me! Listen to me, wildcat!" he ordered, his old imperious self. He squeezed her hands violently, tried to pull her closer. She hung back. Enid sobbed beside her, lost in her own sorrows.

"I will not listen!" stormed Mara, regaining some of her pride. "I will not hear you! You will lie to me—"

"I never lied to you! But I lied to her! Or let her think lies! Listen to me! When I was young and penniless, or nearly so, we were engaged to be married. I was entranced by her beauty; I did not see to the cold selfish person she was beneath the gloss! She flung me over to marry a man in his sixties, a wealthy, gross, corrupt man I despised! Then I knew what she was!"

Mara stared into his eyes. They were blazing blue, furious, and—honest.

"I despised her," he said in a cold tone that told of his renewed fury at the thought. "I felt vast contempt for her, even more so when she came to me and—and offered herself. I turned her down, but in such a way that she would think someday I might—accept. Listen to me, Mara, I despise myself for it. But I led her on, I let her keep thinking I might someday—ah, bah! God, I hate what I did! But it was to punish her. To let her think I still adored her—while all the time I laughed at her greedy, selfish, corrupt self!"

Mara kept staring into his eyes. She ought to be able to tell from his eyes, she thought. But the

cold block of ice was melting inside her, threatening to rise into a flood of river, like the spring
when the warm winds melt the blocks of ice, and
then the floods rise up and sweep like a torrent
over the land.

"You—do—not—love—her?" she whispered.

"Never, never! I love you! I have loved you
from the first, when I saw you in that adorable
blue dress, storming at the dressmaker for making
you look your beautiful self! I loved you, I adored
you! I went crazy when you drove me from you,
oh, Mara! You have made me go through hell! I
thought first José—then Ramón—someone else had
your heart—and I went mad with it!"

"And the affairs—with other women—" she
whispered, still incredulous. She felt faint and dizzy, she could not quite believe yet—

He grimaced. "Over—long ago. Oh, I let my
reputation stand! It was flattering to my vanity.
But after her, after Vivienne—I despised all wom-
en, I thought they were all alike—until you!"

Enid was sobbing quietly now, and Lyman
came over awkwardly to her side and drew her
up. His face was pale, stricken.

"Can you ever forgive me?" Enid sobbed.

"Of course, my love," he said simply. "But I—
I—how can I forgive myself for neglecting you
so?"

That brought on a fresh flood of tears. "Oh, I
can never forgive myself," she sobbed. "I will

change, I promise you, Lyman. I don't deserve you—I am no good at all. I let Mara take the blame—and poor Ramón—his career in danger—"

Mara looked up to see José and Ramón leaving the room, and Enid and Lyman holding to each other in the center of the room. Jennie and Fergus were still watching in great fascination all the living drama before their eyes.

"Oh—there is too much confusion here!" said Gaylord impatiently, and caught up Mara. "Come —up to our rooms, where we can talk in peace! Have you eaten any supper, my love, or did you plan to starve?"

Food, he could think of food! She felt a hysterical giggle in her throat. But he led her imperiously up to their rooms, yelled for Juana who came running. Her maid helped Mara remove the torn, bedraggled blue velvet riding habit, put on a soft nightrobe and negligee, and Gaylord then had trays of food and drink ready for them. And Mara found she was hungry.

They talked then, until almost morning. He insisted on holding her in his arms, comfortably, on the wide couch, talking, listening, hearing all of her doubts and fears.

"And you thought I would desert you, as your father deserted your mother, that was it. And I thought you were in love, first with José, then with Ramón. I could not credit it, that you would melt in my arms at nights—and you did melt, love, I knew that! and then the next day you would treat me with such cold disdain, your little chin so high—" And he cuffed her gently under her rounded silken chin, then kissed it passionately. "Oh, you drove me wild," he breathed against her throat.

She finally roused from her happy dreams in his arms. "But—the deaths tonight, Gaylord. What will happen to us?"

His arms tightened; his face turned more serious. "We shall probably have to leave Spain at once. The embassy will insist on that, I am afraid. Enid and Lyman can close the house and leave—no—because of Ramón, they had best come with us."

"José can be—trusted to close the house," she offered timidly. "I think he would do this."

He smiled down at her tenderly. "Yes, of course he can. He has more care of you than I have! Before we leave, I must discover from him the art of handling you, my little wildcat!" And he drew her up close to him and began kissing her passionately.

She thought he already knew that art—he had from the moment he had set to taming her. His hands made her melt, his kisses set her on fire, and his arms turned her weak and helpless.

They set sail for England within three days. José had agreed to close the house and send their possessions to them. He would then disappear into the countryside, for he meant to join the movement once more. "Spain needs me," he had said gravely. "I am well again. I will give my sword, my wits, my life to make her truly free."

Ramón, full of remorse at the trouble his love-making had brought, and more than a little fearful of the results, Mara thought, had decided to accompany José, whom he deeply admired.

So the others set sail, and on a gray evening Mara stood at the railing and watched the peninsula fade away into the bleak distance. Her Spain, her sunny bright golden Spain, so full of danger, of adventure, of grief—finally of love.

She was standing alone, absorbed in her thoughts, tears stinging her eyes as she watched her beloved land fading. She started when arms went about her, strong possessive arms, folding her cloak more tightly to her as he held her.

"My Mara, do not grieve," Gaylord whispered in her ear. "We shall return here one day, and you shall have your sunny Spain once more! Meantime, I am determined that you shall be happy in England. We shall have a new Casa Dorada there, full of sunshine and flowers and joy. Will that not please you?"

She leaned back in his arms. Her doubts sometimes rose to plague her, but she knew with her mind that she could trust him now. She was safe and secure in her husband's loving care. He was not like her father; he was loyal and good and fine. Her scarred childhood must not be allowed to dim their life together.

"One thing only will please me," she murmured, turning in his arms, turning her back on the land that faded behind her. "One thing—to be with you always—wherever you go—"

She raised her face for his kisses, and her eyes met for a moment the blazing exultant blue of his eyes. She could not become accustomed yet to his love, it was too new and precious, too wild and fierce, though he tried to tame it for her. It warmed her, it dazzled her—just as La Casa Dorada had dazzled and warmed her heart.

She knew she would never forget her first married home, La Casa Dorada. But she carried with her that which made it warm and bright and precious—the man who made it so, and his love.

Dell's Delightful
Candlelight Romances